STAR WARS

EPISODE IV
A NEW HOPE

VOLUME ONE

BASED ON THE STORY SCREENPLAY BY
GEORGE LUCAS

SCRIPT ADAPTATION
BRUCE JONES

PENCILLER
EDUARDO BARRETO

INKERS
**AL WILLIAMSON
EDUARDO BARRETO**

COLORS
JAMES SINCLAIR

LETTERING
STEVE DUTRO

COVER ART AND BACK MATTER ART
DAVE DORMAN

 DARK HORSE COMICS

 Spotlight

VISIT US AT
www.abdopublishing.com

Reinforced library bound edition published in 2010 by Spotlight, a division of the ABDO Group, 8000 West 78th Street, Edina, Minnesota 55439. Spotlight produces high-quality reinforced library bound editions for schools and libraries. Published by agreement with Dark Horse Comics, Inc., and Lucasfilm Ltd.

Library of Congress Cataloging-in-Publication Data

Jones, Bruce, 1944-
   Star wars, episode IV, a new hope / based on the screenplay by George Lucas ; script adaptation Bruce Jones ; penciller Eduardo Barreto ; inkers Al Williamson and Eduardo Barreto ; colors James Sinclair ; lettering Steve Dutro. -- Reinforced library bound ed.
      v. <1-4> cm.
   "Dark Horse."
   ISBN 978-1-59961-621-6 (volume 1) -- ISBN 978-1-59961-622-3 (volume 2) -- ISBN 978-1-59961-623-0 (volume 3) -- ISBN 978-1-59961-624-7 (volume 4)
   1. Graphic novel. I. Lucas, George, 1944- II. Sinclair, James. III. Dutro, Steve. IV. Barreto, Eduardo. V. Williamson, Al, 1939- VI. Dark Horse Comics. VII. Star Wars, episode IV, a new hope (Motion picture) VIII. Title. IX. Title: Star wars, episode four, a new hope. X. Title: Star wars, episode 4, a new hope. XI. Title: New hope.
   PZ7.7.J658Std 2009
   741.5'973--dc22

                    2009002015

All Spotlight books have reinforced library bindings and
are manufactured in the United States of America.

A long time ago in a galaxy far, far away. . . .

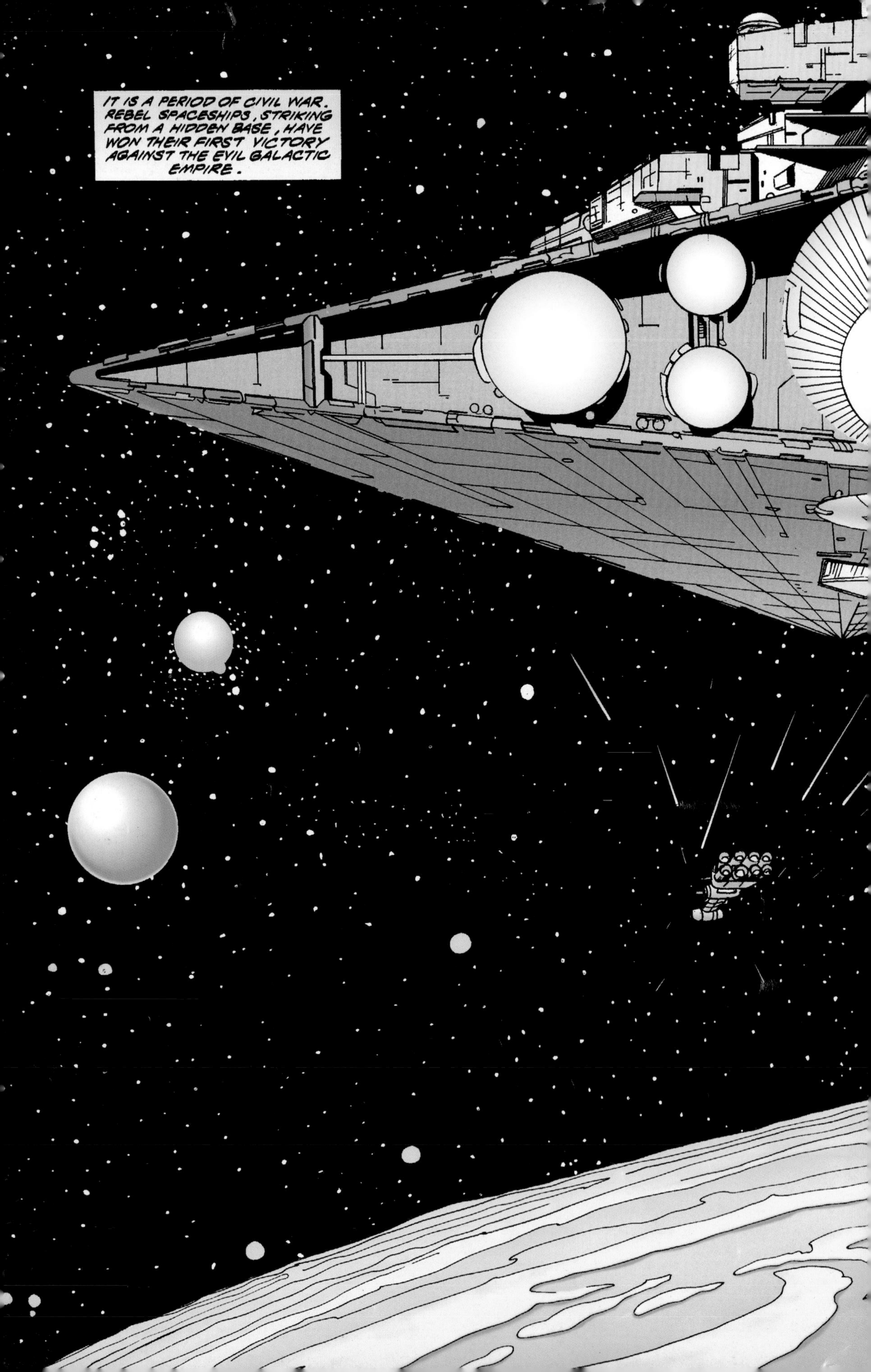
IT IS A PERIOD OF CIVIL WAR. REBEL SPACESHIPS, STRIKING FROM A HIDDEN BASE, HAVE WON THEIR FIRST VICTORY AGAINST THE EVIL GALACTIC EMPIRE.

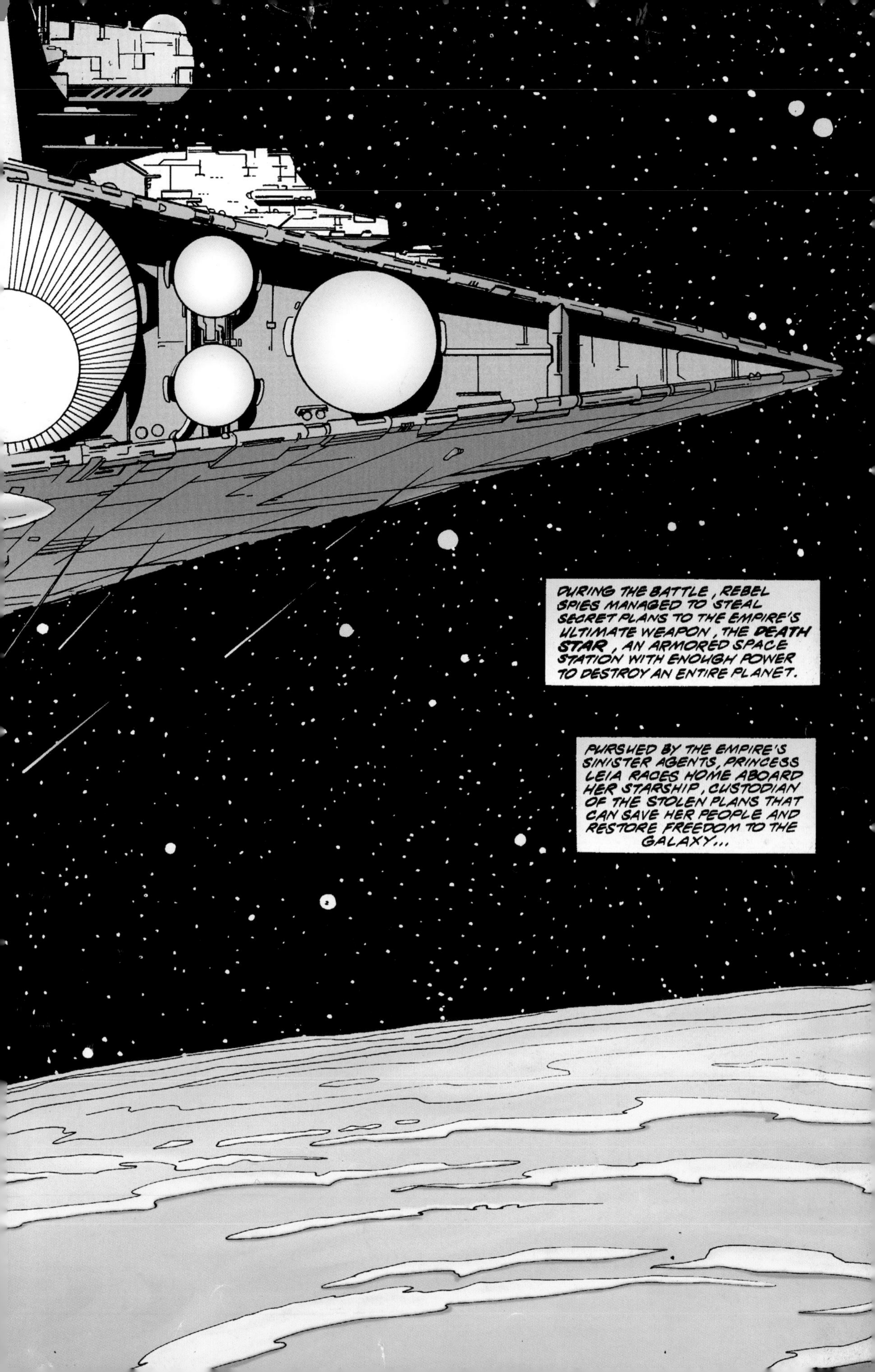
DURING THE BATTLE, REBEL SPIES MANAGED TO STEAL SECRET PLANS TO THE EMPIRE'S ULTIMATE WEAPON, THE DEATH STAR, AN ARMORED SPACE STATION WITH ENOUGH POWER TO DESTROY AN ENTIRE PLANET.
PURSUED BY THE EMPIRE'S SINISTER AGENTS, PRINCESS LEIA RACES HOME ABOARD HER STARSHIP, CUSTODIAN OF THE STOLEN PLANS THAT CAN SAVE HER PEOPLE AND RESTORE FREEDOM TO THE GALAXY...

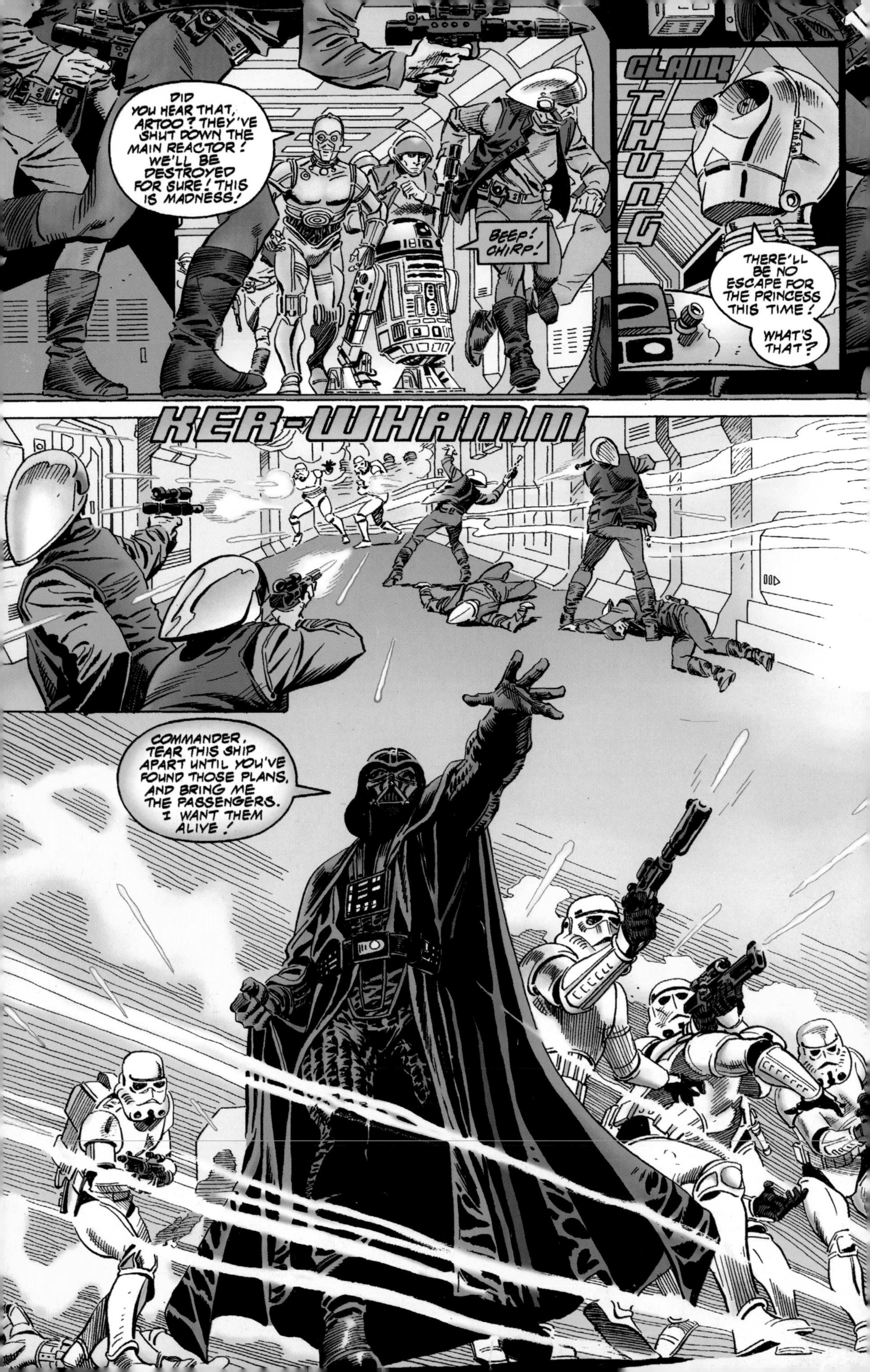
DID YOU HEAR THAT, ARTOO? THEY'VE SHUT DOWN THE MAIN REACTOR! WE'LL BE DESTROYED FOR SURE! THIS IS MADNESS!
BEEP! CHIRP!
CLANK
THUNG
THERE'LL BE NO ESCAPE FOR THE PRINCESS THIS TIME!
WHAT'S THAT?
KER-WHAMM
COMMANDER, TEAR THIS SHIP APART UNTIL YOU'VE FOUND THOSE PLANS, AND BRING ME THE PASSENGERS. I WANT THEM ALIVE!

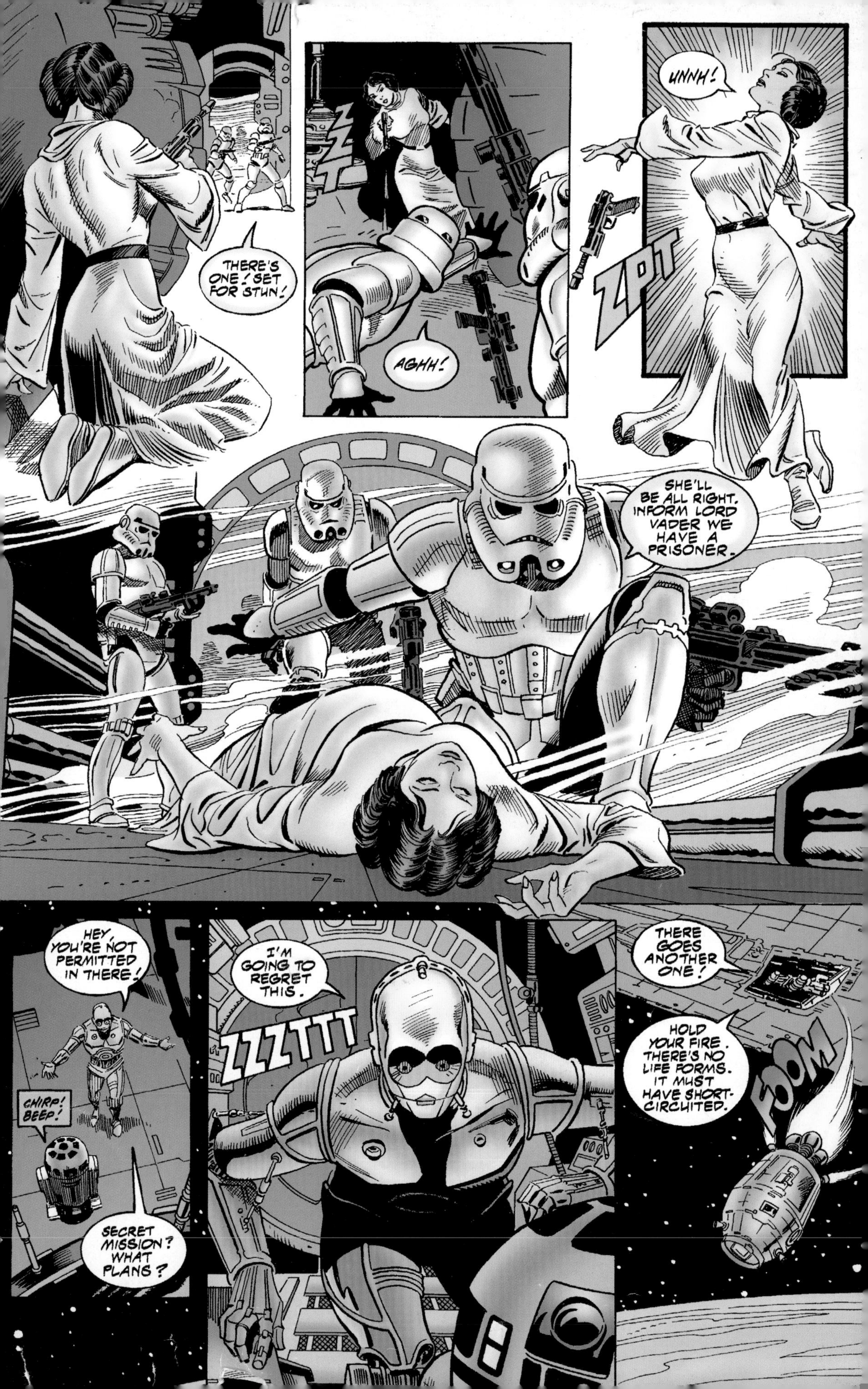
THERE'S ONE! SET FOR STUN!
ZZT
AGHH!
UNNH!
ZPT
SHE'LL BE ALL RIGHT. INFORM LORD VADER WE HAVE A PRISONER.
HEY, YOU'RE NOT PERMITTED IN THERE!
CHIRP! BEEP!
SECRET MISSION? WHAT PLANS?
I'M GOING TO REGRET THIS.
ZZZTTT
THERE GOES ANOTHER ONE!
HOLD YOUR FIRE. THERE'S NO LIFE FORMS. IT MUST HAVE SHORT-CIRCUITED.
FOOM

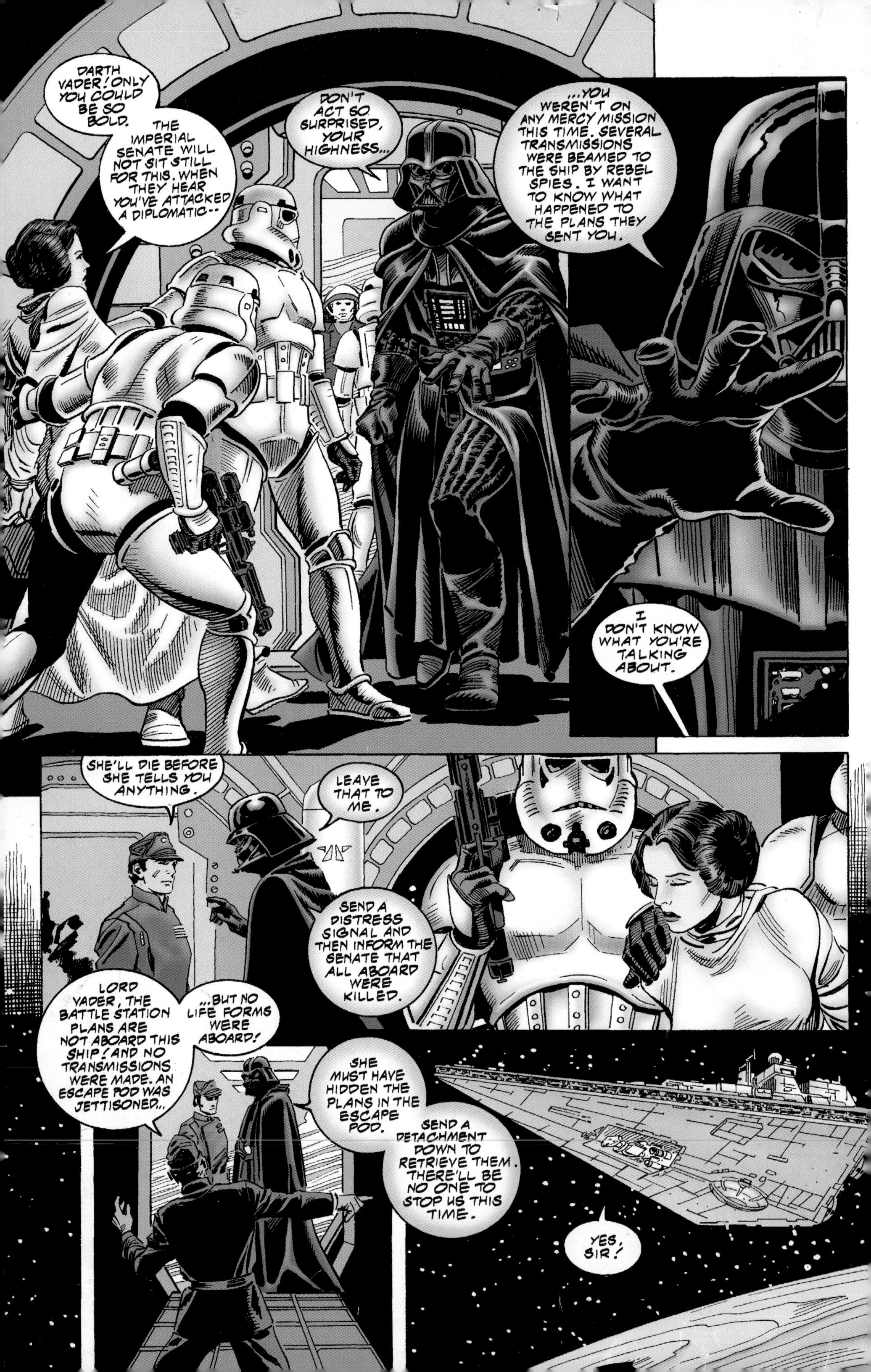
DARTH VADER! ONLY YOU COULD BE SO BOLD.
THE IMPERIAL SENATE WILL NOT SIT STILL FOR THIS. WHEN THEY HEAR YOU'VE ATTACKED A DIPLOMATIC--
DON'T ACT SO SURPRISED, YOUR HIGHNESS...
...YOU WEREN'T ON ANY MERCY MISSION THIS TIME. SEVERAL TRANSMISSIONS WERE BEAMED TO THE SHIP BY REBEL SPIES. I WANT TO KNOW WHAT HAPPENED TO THE PLANS THEY SENT YOU.
I DON'T KNOW WHAT YOU'RE TALKING ABOUT.
SHE'LL DIE BEFORE SHE TELLS YOU ANYTHING.
LEAVE THAT TO ME.
SEND A DISTRESS SIGNAL AND THEN INFORM THE SENATE THAT ALL ABOARD WERE KILLED.
LORD VADER, THE BATTLE STATION PLANS ARE NOT ABOARD THIS SHIP! AND NO TRANSMISSIONS WERE MADE. AN ESCAPE POD WAS JETTISONED...
...BUT NO LIFE FORMS WERE ABOARD!
SHE MUST HAVE HIDDEN THE PLANS IN THE ESCAPE POD.
SEND A DETACHMENT DOWN TO RETRIEVE THEM. THERE'LL BE NO ONE TO STOP US THIS TIME.
YES, SIR!

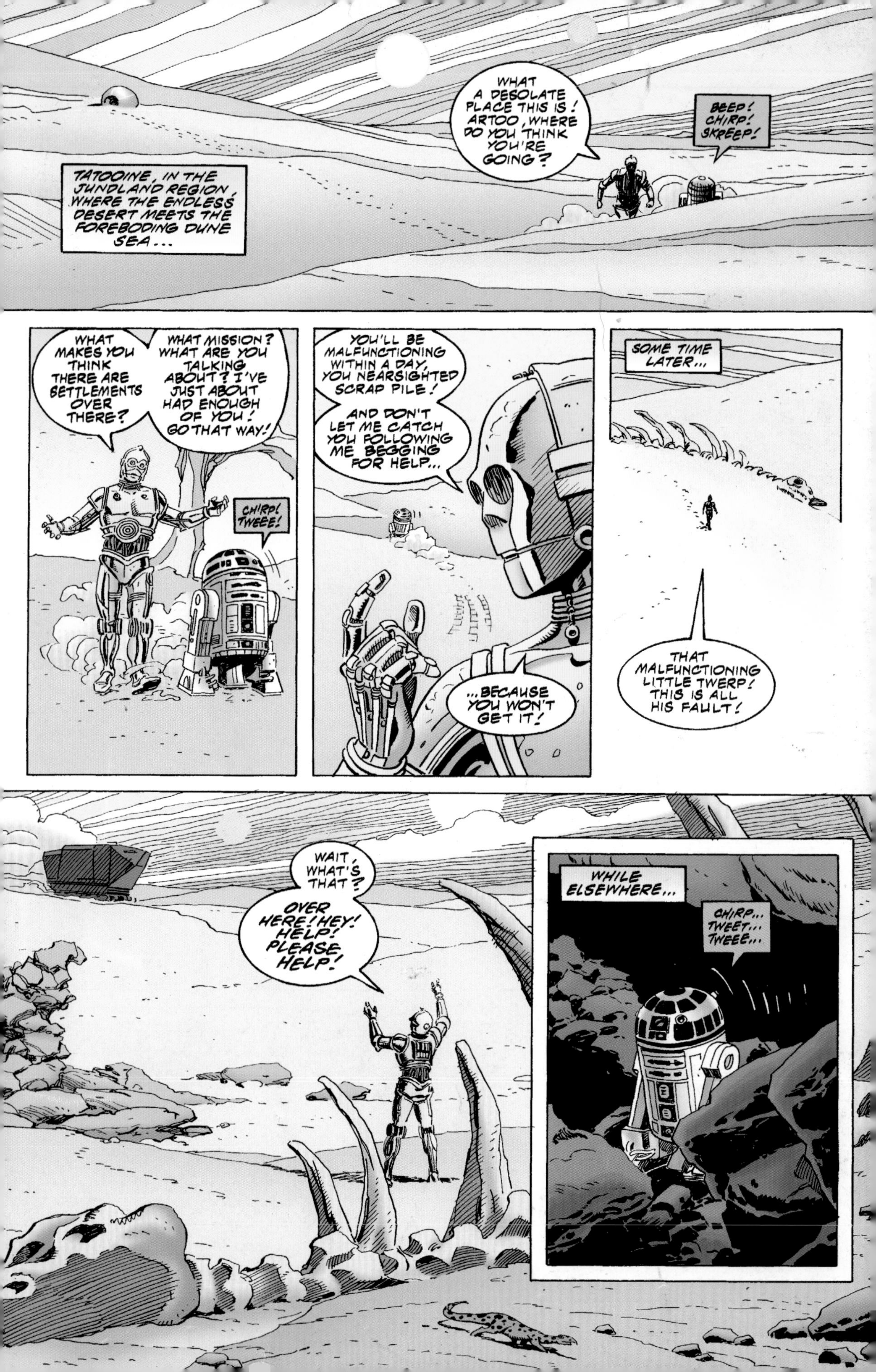
TATOOINE, IN THE JUNDLAND REGION, WHERE THE ENDLESS DESERT MEETS THE FOREBODING DUNE SEA...
WHAT A DESOLATE PLACE THIS IS! ARTOO, WHERE DO YOU THINK YOU'RE GOING?
BEEP! CHIRP! SKREEP!
WHAT MAKES YOU THINK THERE ARE SETTLEMENTS OVER THERE?
WHAT MISSION? WHAT ARE YOU TALKING ABOUT? I'VE JUST ABOUT HAD ENOUGH OF YOU! GO THAT WAY!
CHIRP! TWEEE!
YOU'LL BE MALFUNCTIONING WITHIN A DAY, YOU NEARSIGHTED SCRAP PILE!
AND DON'T LET ME CATCH YOU FOLLOWING ME BEGGING FOR HELP...
...BECAUSE YOU WON'T GET IT!
SOME TIME LATER...
THAT MALFUNCTIONING LITTLE TWERP! THIS IS ALL HIS FAULT!
WAIT, WHAT'S THAT?
OVER HERE! HEY! HELP! PLEASE, HELP!
WHILE ELSEWHERE...
CHIRP... TWEET... TWEEE...

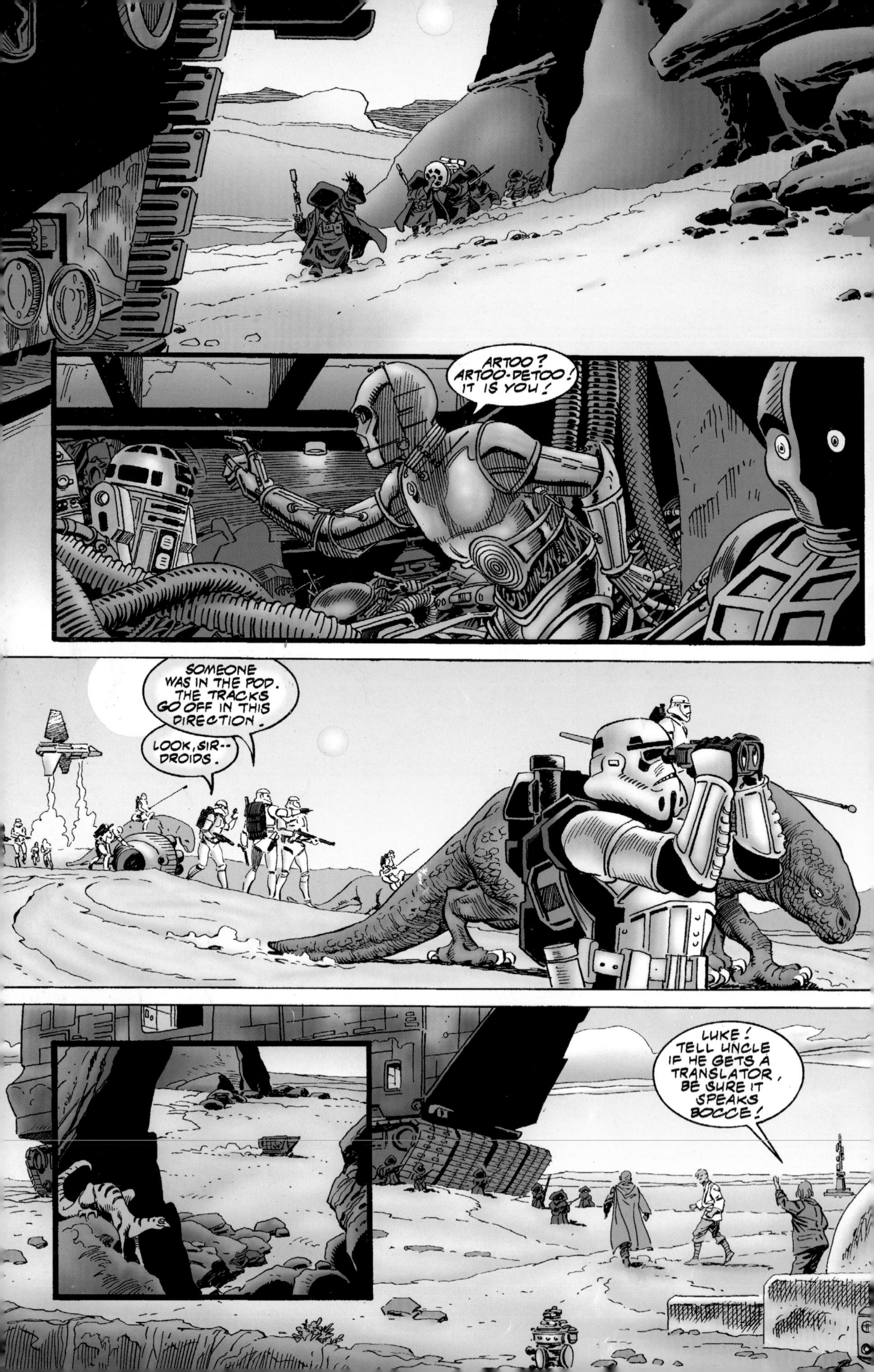
ARTOO? ARTOO-DETOO! IT IS YOU!
SOMEONE WAS IN THE POD. THE TRACKS GO OFF IN THIS DIRECTION.
LOOK, SIR-- DROIDS.
LUKE! TELL UNCLE IF HE GETS A TRANSLATOR, BE SURE IT SPEAKS BOCCE!

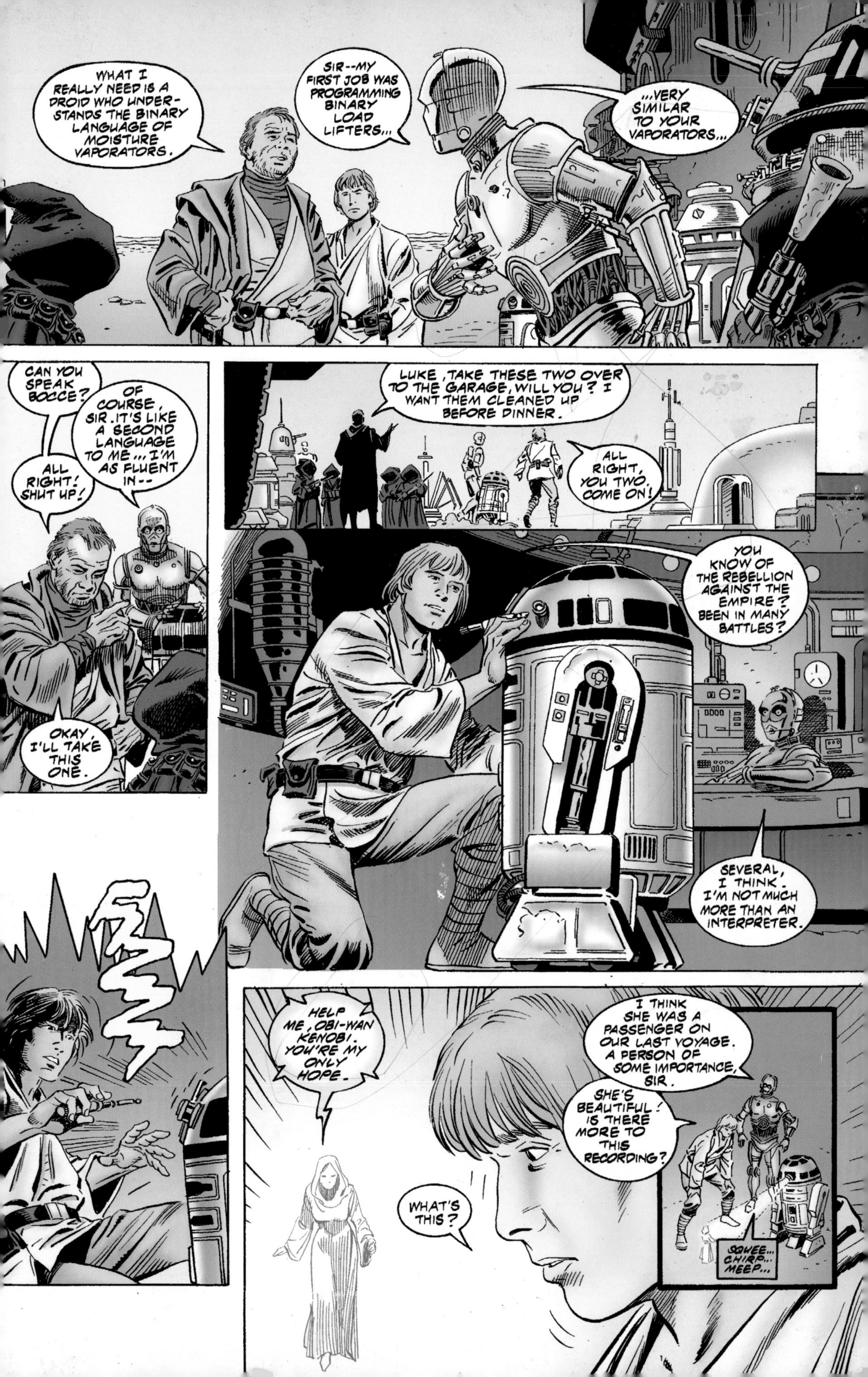
WHAT I REALLY NEED IS A DROID WHO UNDER-STANDS THE BINARY LANGUAGE OF MOISTURE VAPORATORS.
SIR--MY FIRST JOB WAS PROGRAMMING BINARY LOAD LIFTERS...
...VERY SIMILAR TO YOUR VAPORATORS...
CAN YOU SPEAK BOCCE?
OF COURSE, SIR. IT'S LIKE A SECOND LANGUAGE TO ME... I'M AS FLUENT IN--
ALL RIGHT! SHUT UP!
OKAY, I'LL TAKE THIS ONE.
LUKE, TAKE THESE TWO OVER TO THE GARAGE, WILL YOU? I WANT THEM CLEANED UP BEFORE DINNER.
ALL RIGHT, YOU TWO, COME ON!
YOU KNOW OF THE REBELLION AGAINST THE EMPIRE? BEEN IN MANY BATTLES?
SEVERAL, I THINK. I'M NOT MUCH MORE THAN AN INTERPRETER.
HELP ME, OBI-WAN KENOBI. YOU'RE MY ONLY HOPE.
WHAT'S THIS?
I THINK SHE WAS A PASSENGER ON OUR LAST VOYAGE. A PERSON OF SOME IMPORTANCE, SIR.
SHE'S BEAUTIFUL! IS THERE MORE TO THIS RECORDING?
SQUEE... CHIRP... MEEP...

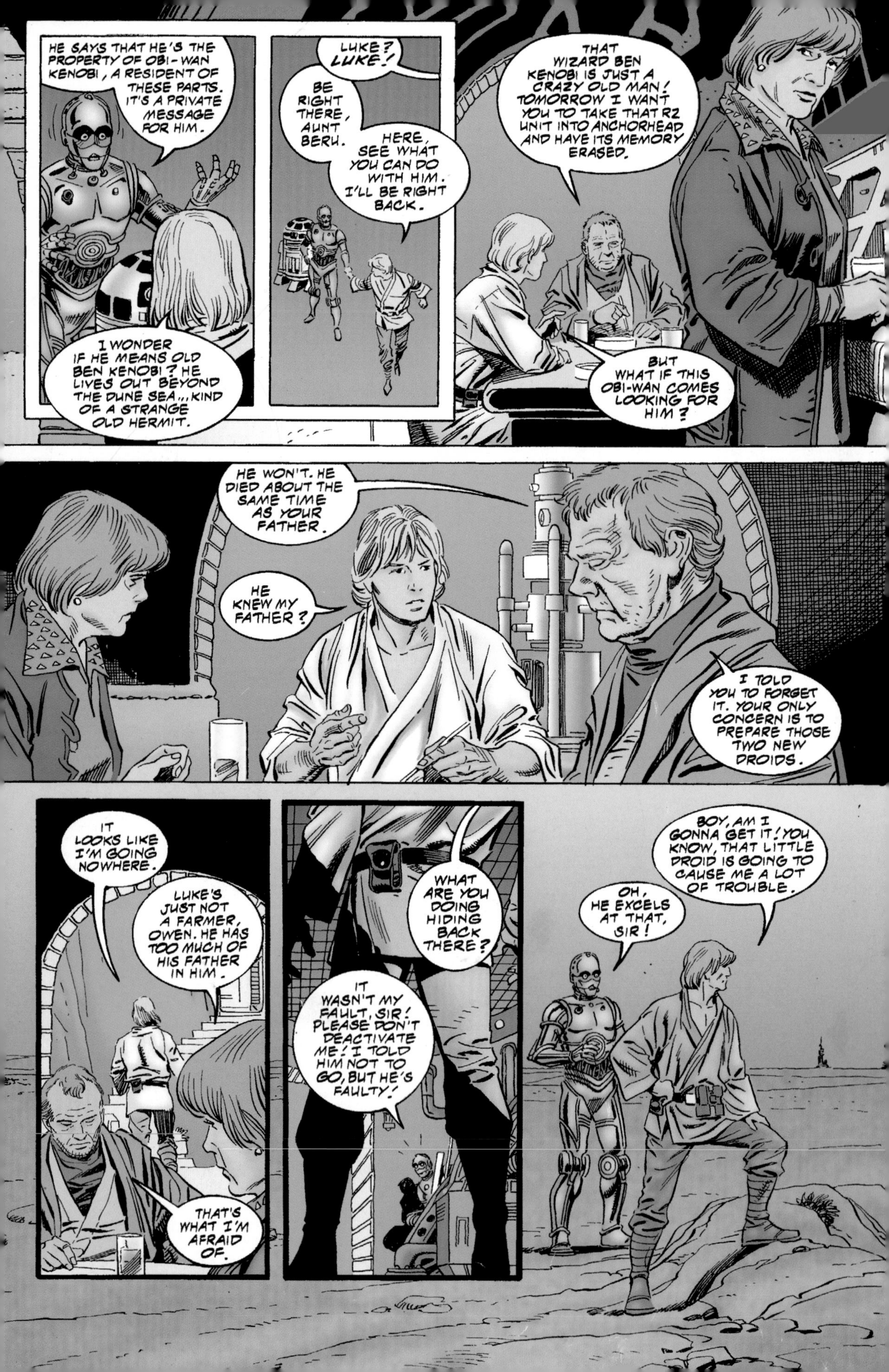

HE SAYS THAT HE'S THE PROPERTY OF OBI-WAN KENOBI, A RESIDENT OF THESE PARTS. IT'S A PRIVATE MESSAGE FOR HIM.
I WONDER IF HE MEANS OLD BEN KENOBI? HE LIVES OUT BEYOND THE DUNE SEA... KIND OF A STRANGE OLD HERMIT.
LUKE? LUKE!
BE RIGHT THERE, AUNT BERU.
HERE, SEE WHAT YOU CAN DO WITH HIM. I'LL BE RIGHT BACK.
THAT WIZARD BEN KENOBI IS JUST A CRAZY OLD MAN! TOMORROW I WANT YOU TO TAKE THAT R2 UNIT INTO ANCHORHEAD AND HAVE ITS MEMORY ERASED.
BUT WHAT IF THIS OBI-WAN COMES LOOKING FOR HIM?
HE WON'T. HE DIED ABOUT THE SAME TIME AS YOUR FATHER.
HE KNEW MY FATHER?
I TOLD YOU TO FORGET IT. YOUR ONLY CONCERN IS TO PREPARE THOSE TWO NEW DROIDS.
IT LOOKS LIKE I'M GOING NOWHERE.
LUKE'S JUST NOT A FARMER, OWEN. HE HAS TOO MUCH OF HIS FATHER IN HIM.
THAT'S WHAT I'M AFRAID OF.
WHAT ARE YOU DOING HIDING BACK THERE?
IT WASN'T MY FAULT, SIR! PLEASE DON'T DEACTIVATE ME! I TOLD HIM NOT TO GO, BUT HE'S FAULTY!
BOY, AM I GONNA GET IT! YOU KNOW, THAT LITTLE DROID IS GOING TO CAUSE ME A LOT OF TROUBLE.
OH, HE EXCELS AT THAT, SIR!

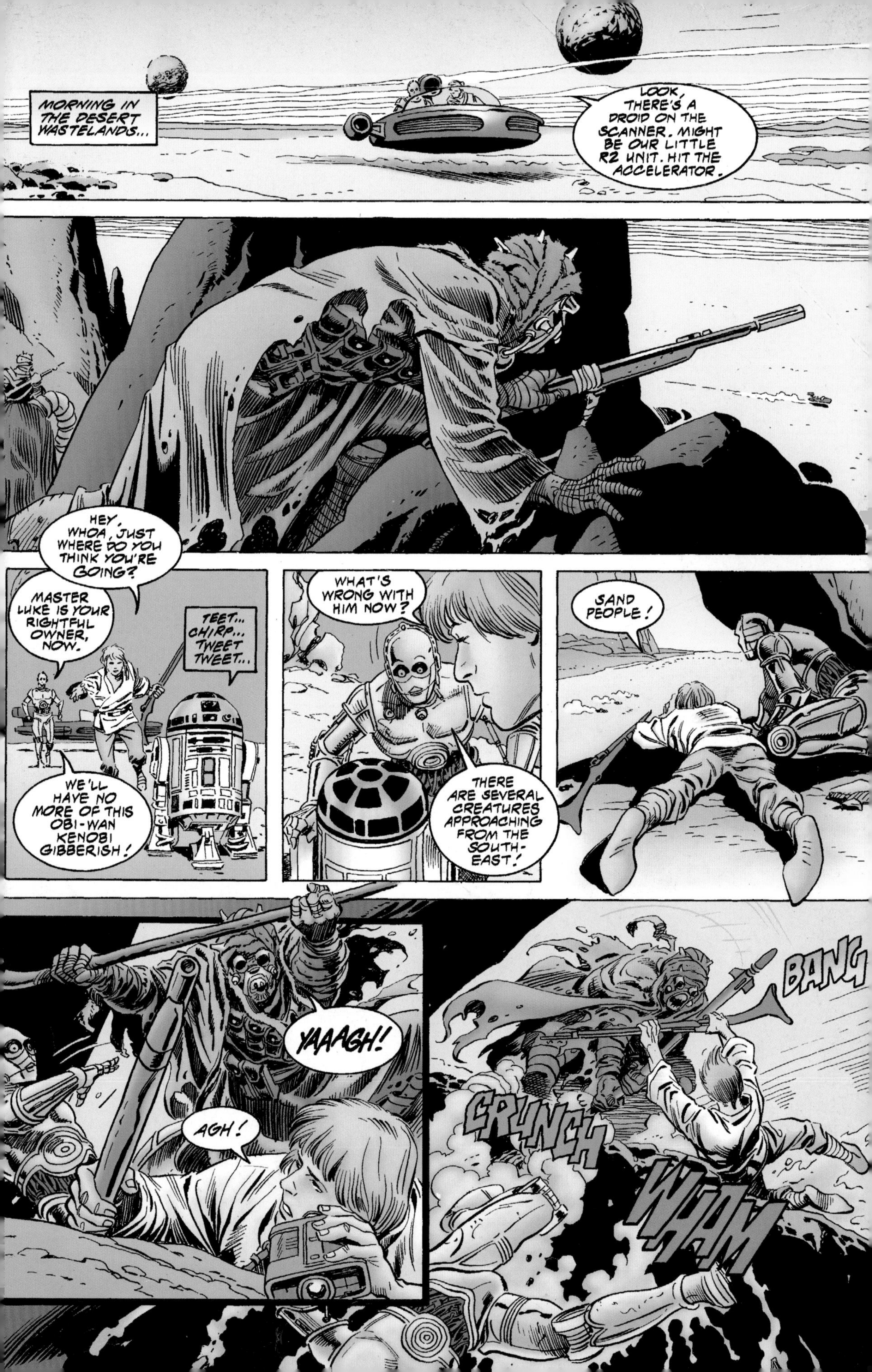
MORNING IN THE DESERT WASTELANDS...
LOOK, THERE'S A DROID ON THE SCANNER. MIGHT BE OUR LITTLE R2 UNIT. HIT THE ACCELERATOR.
HEY, WHOA, JUST WHERE DO YOU THINK YOU'RE GOING?
MASTER LUKE IS YOUR RIGHTFUL OWNER, NOW.
TEET... CHIRP... TWEET TWEET...
WE'LL HAVE NO MORE OF THIS OBI-WAN KENOBI GIBBERISH!
WHAT'S WRONG WITH HIM NOW?
THERE ARE SEVERAL CREATURES APPROACHING FROM THE SOUTH-EAST!
SAND PEOPLE!
YAAAGH!
AGH!
BANG
CRUNCH
WHAM

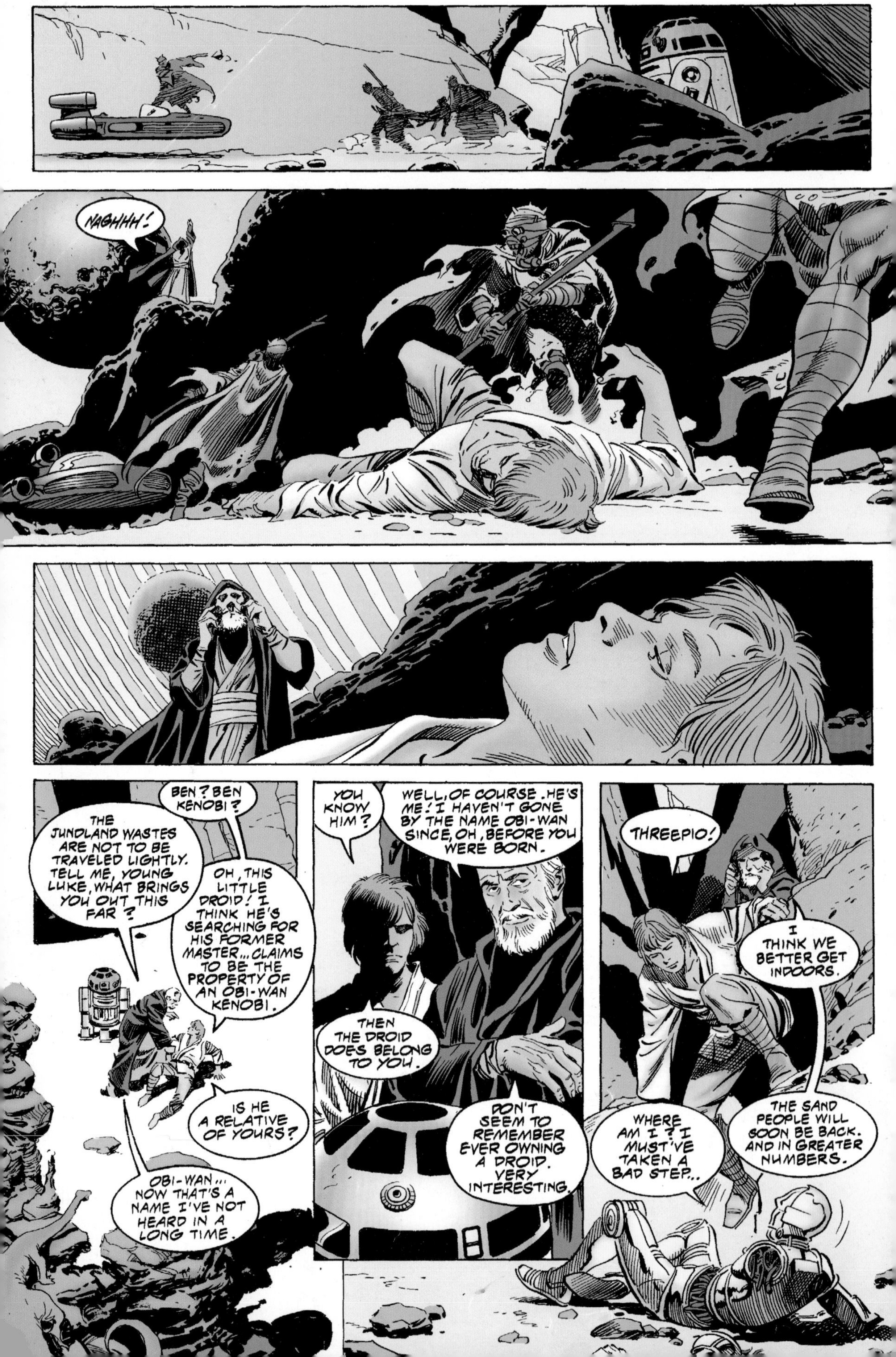
NAGHHH!
THE JUNDLAND WASTES ARE NOT TO BE TRAVELED LIGHTLY. TELL ME, YOUNG LUKE, WHAT BRINGS YOU OUT THIS FAR?
BEN? BEN KENOBI?
OH, THIS LITTLE DROID! I THINK HE'S SEARCHING FOR HIS FORMER MASTER... CLAIMS TO BE THE PROPERTY OF AN OBI-WAN KENOBI.
IS HE A RELATIVE OF YOURS?
OBI-WAN... NOW THAT'S A NAME I'VE NOT HEARD IN A LONG TIME.
YOU KNOW HIM?
WELL, OF COURSE. HE'S ME! I HAVEN'T GONE BY THE NAME OBI-WAN SINCE, OH, BEFORE YOU WERE BORN.
THEN THE DROID DOES BELONG TO YOU.
DON'T SEEM TO REMEMBER EVER OWNING A DROID. VERY INTERESTING.
THREEPIO!
I THINK WE BETTER GET INDOORS.
THE SAND PEOPLE WILL SOON BE BACK. AND IN GREATER NUMBERS.
WHERE AM I? I MUST'VE TAKEN A BAD STEP...

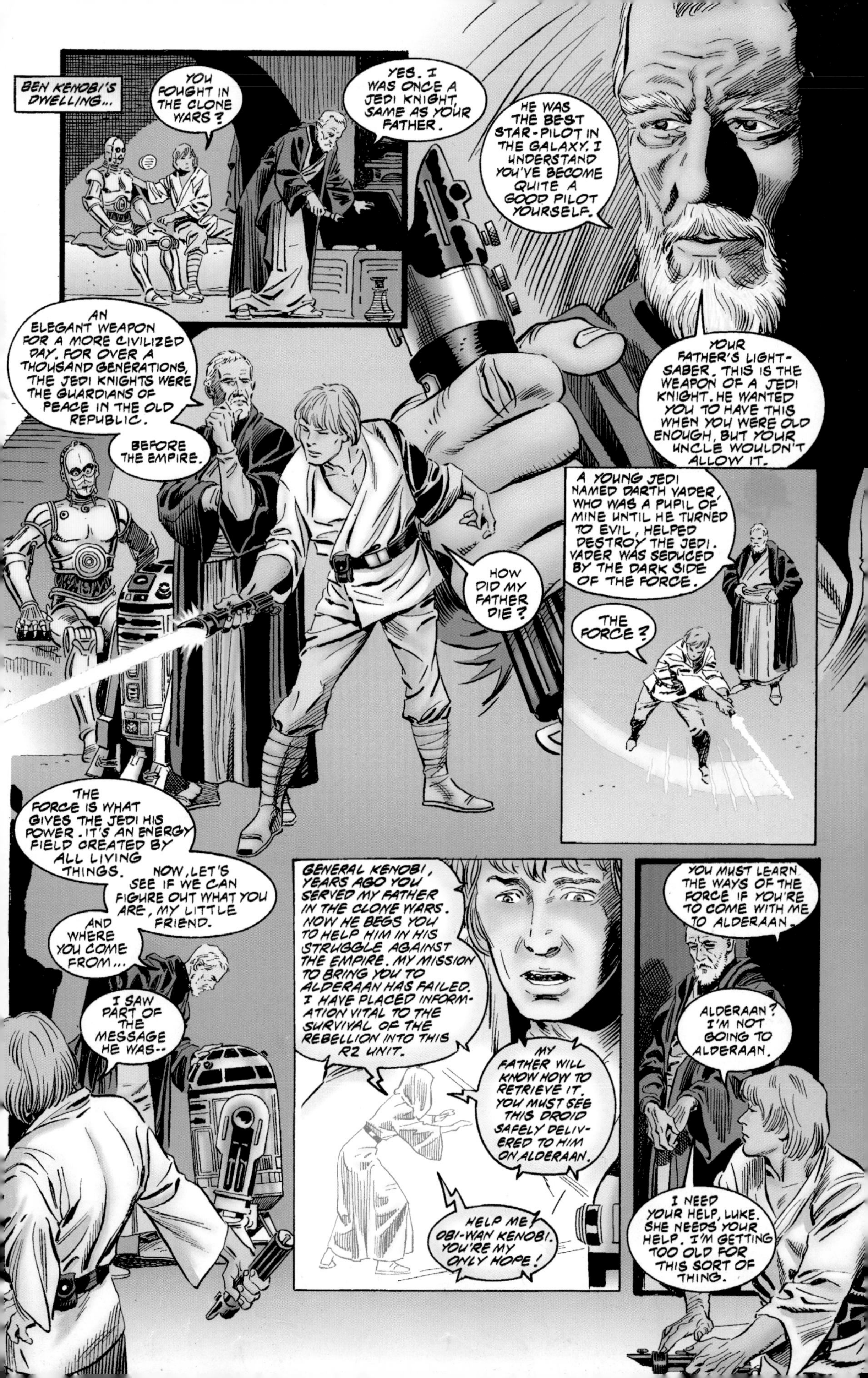

BEN KENOBI'S DWELLING...
YOU FOUGHT IN THE CLONE WARS?
YES. I WAS ONCE A JEDI KNIGHT, SAME AS YOUR FATHER.
HE WAS THE BEST STAR-PILOT IN THE GALAXY. I UNDERSTAND YOU'VE BECOME QUITE A GOOD PILOT YOURSELF.
YOUR FATHER'S LIGHT-SABER. THIS IS THE WEAPON OF A JEDI KNIGHT. HE WANTED YOU TO HAVE THIS WHEN YOU WERE OLD ENOUGH, BUT YOUR UNCLE WOULDN'T ALLOW IT.
AN ELEGANT WEAPON FOR A MORE CIVILIZED DAY. FOR OVER A THOUSAND GENERATIONS, THE JEDI KNIGHTS WERE THE GUARDIANS OF PEACE IN THE OLD REPUBLIC.
BEFORE THE EMPIRE.
HOW DID MY FATHER DIE?
A YOUNG JEDI NAMED DARTH VADER, WHO WAS A PUPIL OF MINE UNTIL HE TURNED TO EVIL, HELPED DESTROY THE JEDI. VADER WAS SEDUCED BY THE DARK SIDE OF THE FORCE.
THE FORCE?
THE FORCE IS WHAT GIVES THE JEDI HIS POWER. IT'S AN ENERGY FIELD CREATED BY ALL LIVING THINGS.
NOW, LET'S SEE IF WE CAN FIGURE OUT WHAT YOU ARE, MY LITTLE FRIEND.
AND WHERE YOU COME FROM...
I SAW PART OF THE MESSAGE HE WAS--
GENERAL KENOBI, YEARS AGO YOU SERVED MY FATHER IN THE CLONE WARS. NOW HE BEGS YOU TO HELP HIM IN HIS STRUGGLE AGAINST THE EMPIRE. MY MISSION TO BRING YOU TO ALDERAAN HAS FAILED. I HAVE PLACED INFORMATION VITAL TO THE SURVIVAL OF THE REBELLION INTO THIS R2 UNIT.
MY FATHER WILL KNOW HOW TO RETRIEVE IT. YOU MUST SEE THIS DROID SAFELY DELIVERED TO HIM ON ALDERAAN.
HELP ME! OBI-WAN KENOBI. YOU'RE MY ONLY HOPE!
YOU MUST LEARN THE WAYS OF THE FORCE IF YOU'RE TO COME WITH ME TO ALDERAAN.
ALDERAAN? I'M NOT GOING TO ALDERAAN.
I NEED YOUR HELP, LUKE. SHE NEEDS YOUR HELP. I'M GETTING TOO OLD FOR THIS SORT OF THING.

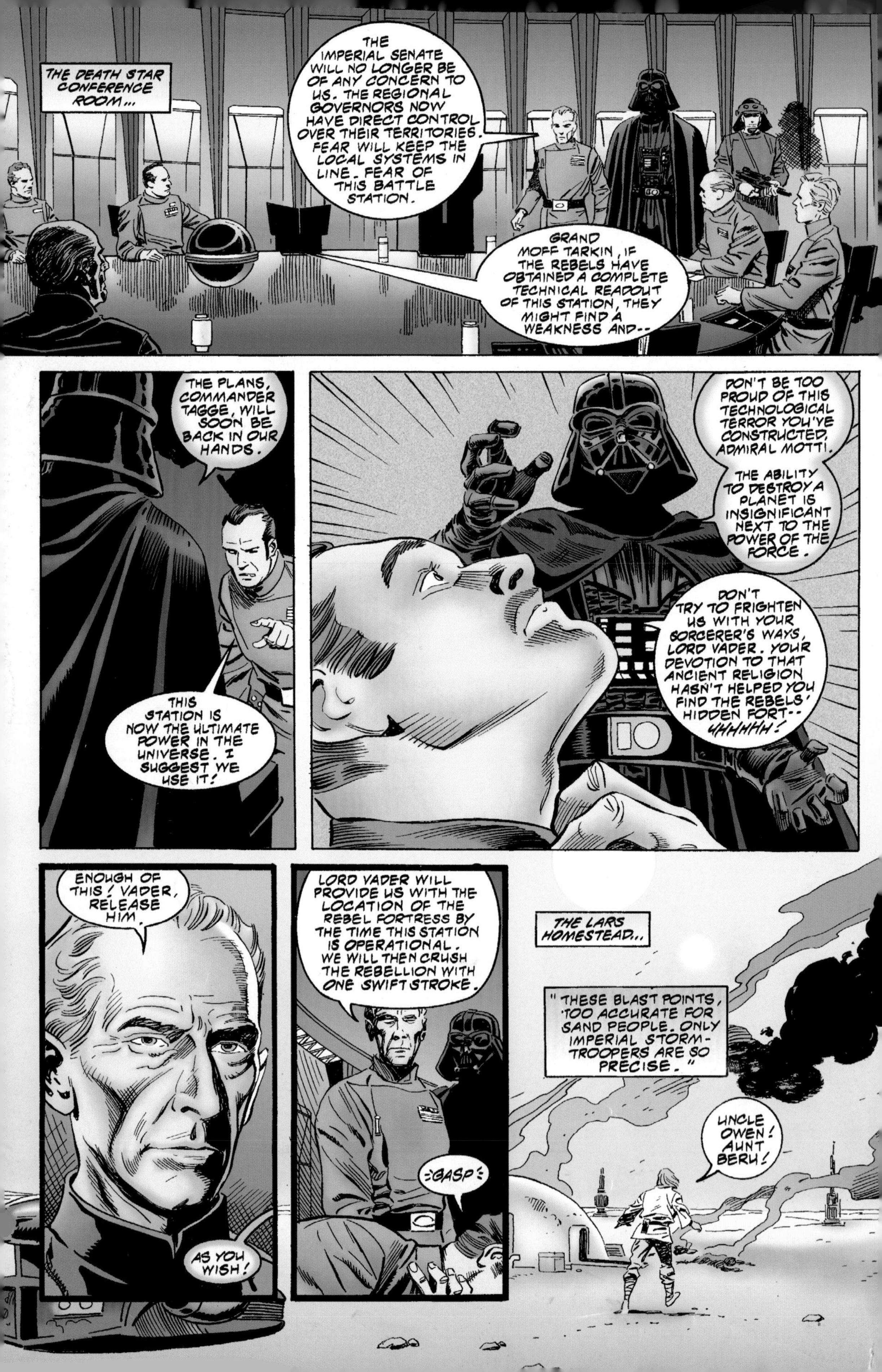
THE DEATH STAR CONFERENCE ROOM...
THE IMPERIAL SENATE WILL NO LONGER BE OF ANY CONCERN TO US. THE REGIONAL GOVERNORS NOW HAVE DIRECT CONTROL OVER THEIR TERRITORIES. FEAR WILL KEEP THE LOCAL SYSTEMS IN LINE. FEAR OF THIS BATTLE STATION.
GRAND MOFF TARKIN, IF THE REBELS HAVE OBTAINED A COMPLETE TECHNICAL READOUT OF THIS STATION, THEY MIGHT FIND A WEAKNESS AND--
THE PLANS, COMMANDER TAGGE, WILL SOON BE BACK IN OUR HANDS.
THIS STATION IS NOW THE ULTIMATE POWER IN THE UNIVERSE. I SUGGEST WE USE IT!
DON'T BE TOO PROUD OF THIS TECHNOLOGICAL TERROR YOU'VE CONSTRUCTED, ADMIRAL MOTTI.
THE ABILITY TO DESTROY A PLANET IS INSIGNIFICANT NEXT TO THE POWER OF THE FORCE.
DON'T TRY TO FRIGHTEN US WITH YOUR SORCERER'S WAYS, LORD VADER. YOUR DEVOTION TO THAT ANCIENT RELIGION HASN'T HELPED YOU FIND THE REBELS' HIDDEN FORT-- UHHHHH!
ENOUGH OF THIS! VADER, RELEASE HIM.
AS YOU WISH!
LORD VADER WILL PROVIDE US WITH THE LOCATION OF THE REBEL FORTRESS BY THE TIME THIS STATION IS OPERATIONAL. WE WILL THEN CRUSH THE REBELLION WITH ONE SWIFT STROKE.
:GASP:
THE LARS HOMESTEAD...
"THESE BLAST POINTS, TOO ACCURATE FOR SAND PEOPLE. ONLY IMPERIAL STORM-TROOPERS ARE SO PRECISE."
UNCLE OWEN! AUNT BERU!

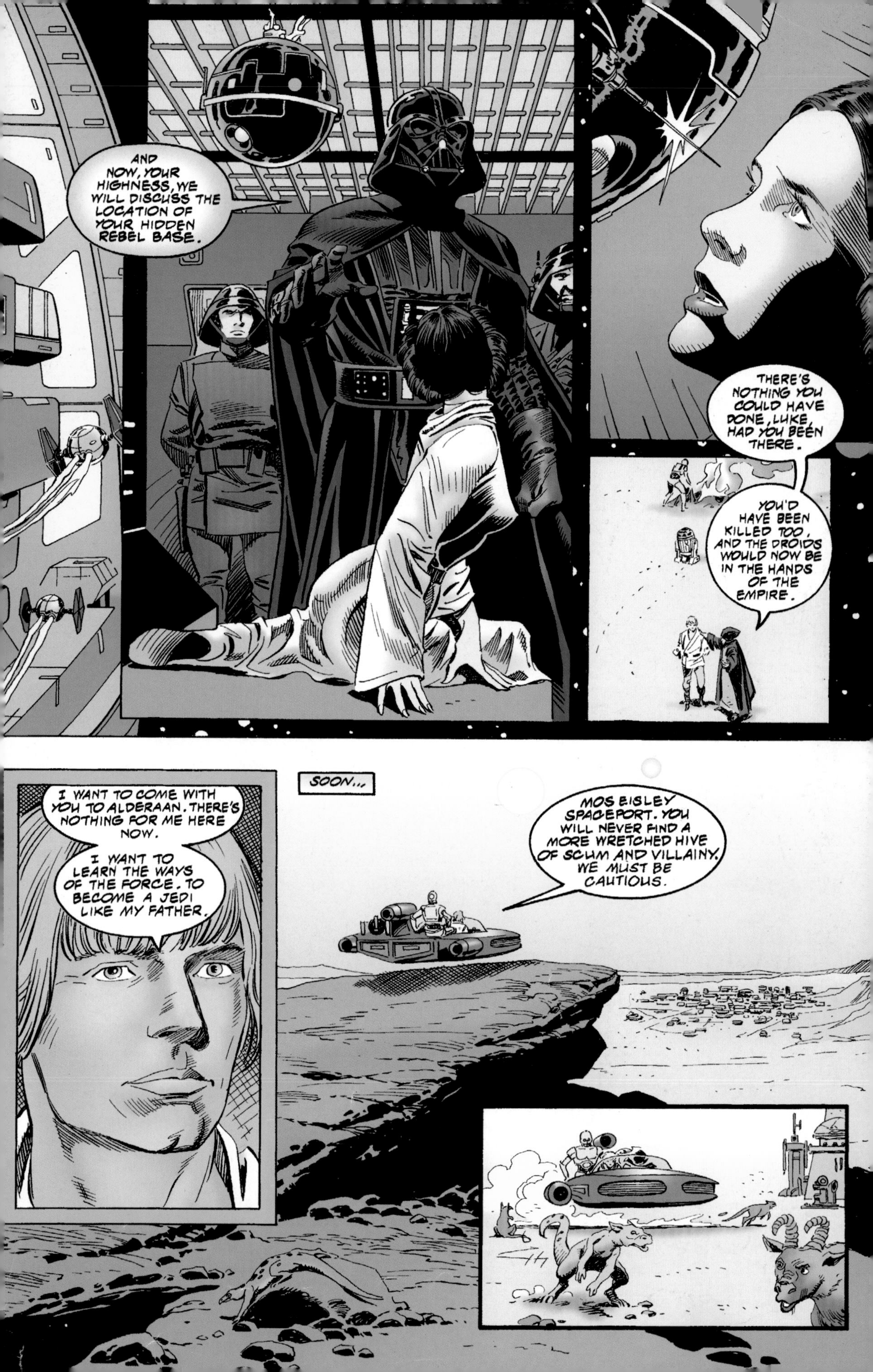
AND NOW, YOUR HIGHNESS, WE WILL DISCUSS THE LOCATION OF YOUR HIDDEN REBEL BASE.
THERE'S NOTHING YOU COULD HAVE DONE, LUKE, HAD YOU BEEN THERE.
YOU'D HAVE BEEN KILLED TOO, AND THE DROIDS WOULD NOW BE IN THE HANDS OF THE EMPIRE.
I WANT TO COME WITH YOU TO ALDERAAN. THERE'S NOTHING FOR ME HERE NOW.
I WANT TO LEARN THE WAYS OF THE FORCE. TO BECOME A JEDI LIKE MY FATHER.
SOON...
MOS EISLEY SPACEPORT. YOU WILL NEVER FIND A MORE WRETCHED HIVE OF SCUM AND VILLAINY. WE MUST BE CAUTIOUS.

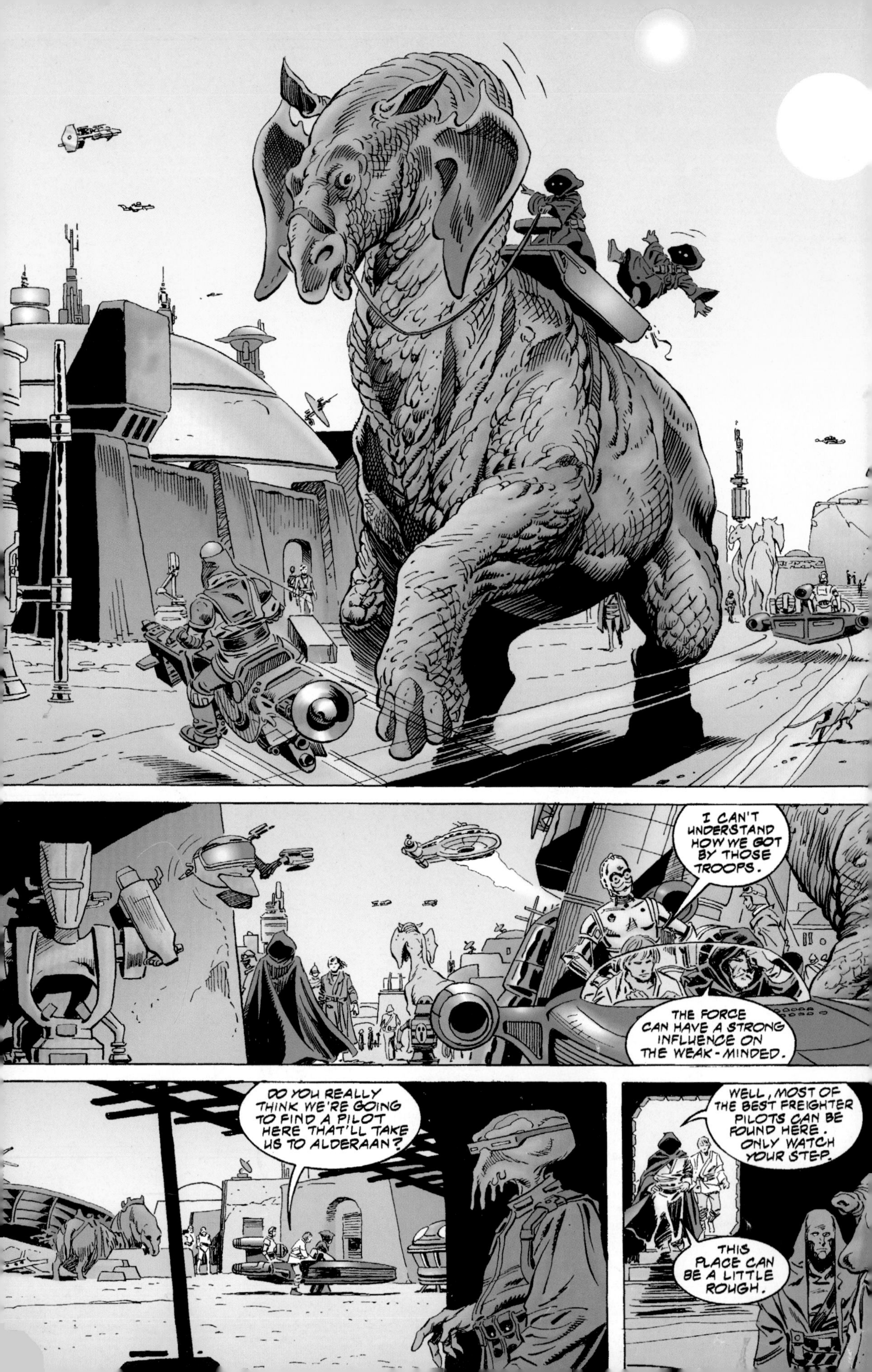
I CAN'T UNDERSTAND HOW WE GOT BY THOSE TROOPS.
THE FORCE CAN HAVE A STRONG INFLUENCE ON THE WEAK-MINDED.
DO YOU REALLY THINK WE'RE GOING TO FIND A PILOT HERE THAT'LL TAKE US TO ALDERAAN?
WELL, MOST OF THE BEST FREIGHTER PILOTS CAN BE FOUND HERE. ONLY WATCH YOUR STEP.
THIS PLACE CAN BE A LITTLE ROUGH.

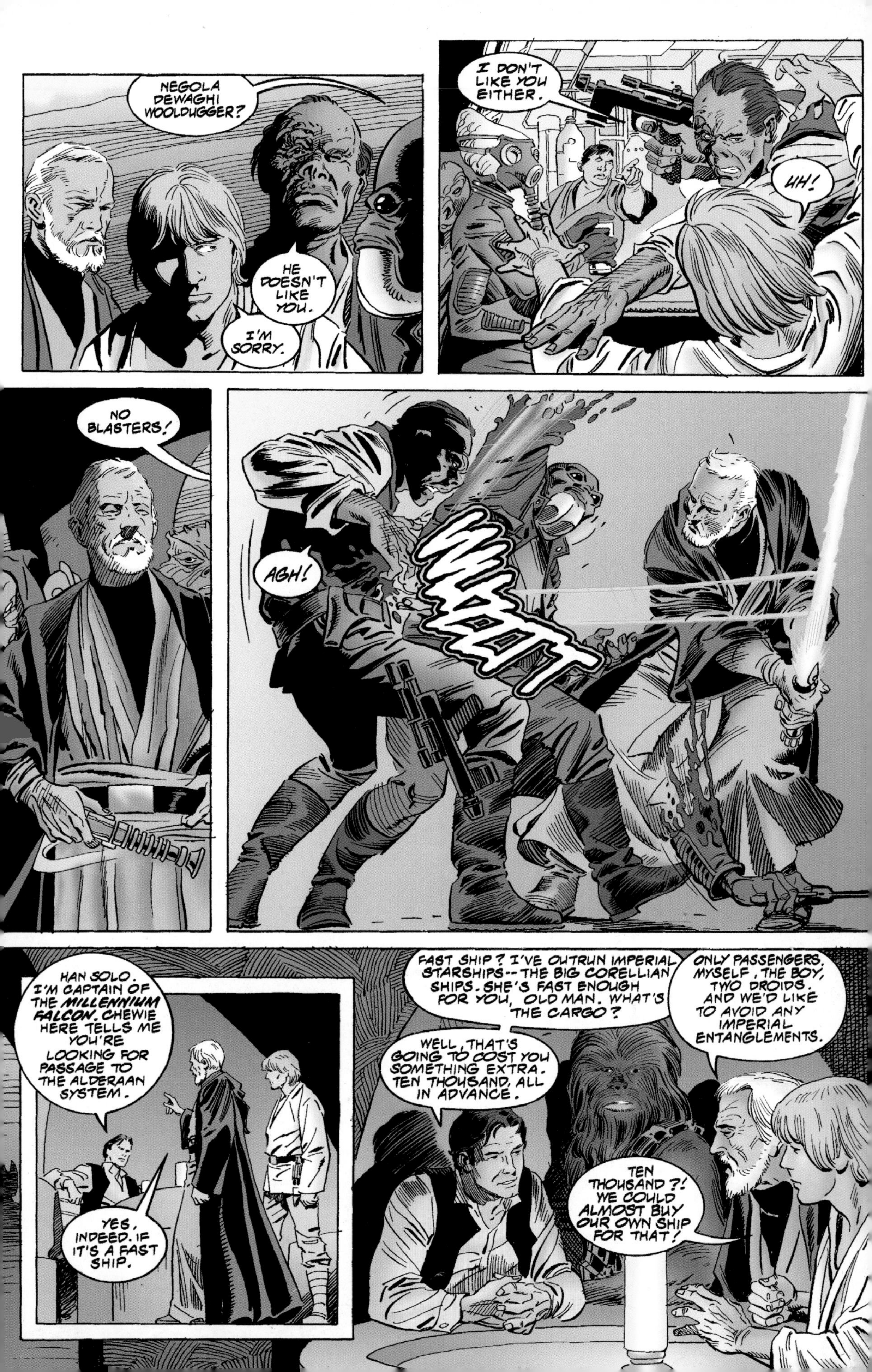
NEGOLA DEWAGHI WOOLDUGGER?
HE DOESN'T LIKE YOU.
I'M SORRY.
I DON'T LIKE YOU EITHER.
UH!
NO BLASTERS!
AGH!
HAN SOLO. I'M CAPTAIN OF THE MILLENNIUM FALCON. CHEWIE HERE TELLS ME YOU'RE LOOKING FOR PASSAGE TO THE ALDERAAN SYSTEM.
YES, INDEED. IF IT'S A FAST SHIP.
FAST SHIP? I'VE OUTRUN IMPERIAL STARSHIPS-- THE BIG CORELLIAN SHIPS. SHE'S FAST ENOUGH FOR YOU, OLD MAN. WHAT'S THE CARGO?
ONLY PASSENGERS. MYSELF, THE BOY, TWO DROIDS. AND WE'D LIKE TO AVOID ANY IMPERIAL ENTANGLEMENTS.
WELL, THAT'S GOING TO COST YOU SOMETHING EXTRA. TEN THOUSAND, ALL IN ADVANCE.
TEN THOUSAND?! WE COULD ALMOST BUY OUR OWN SHIP FOR THAT!

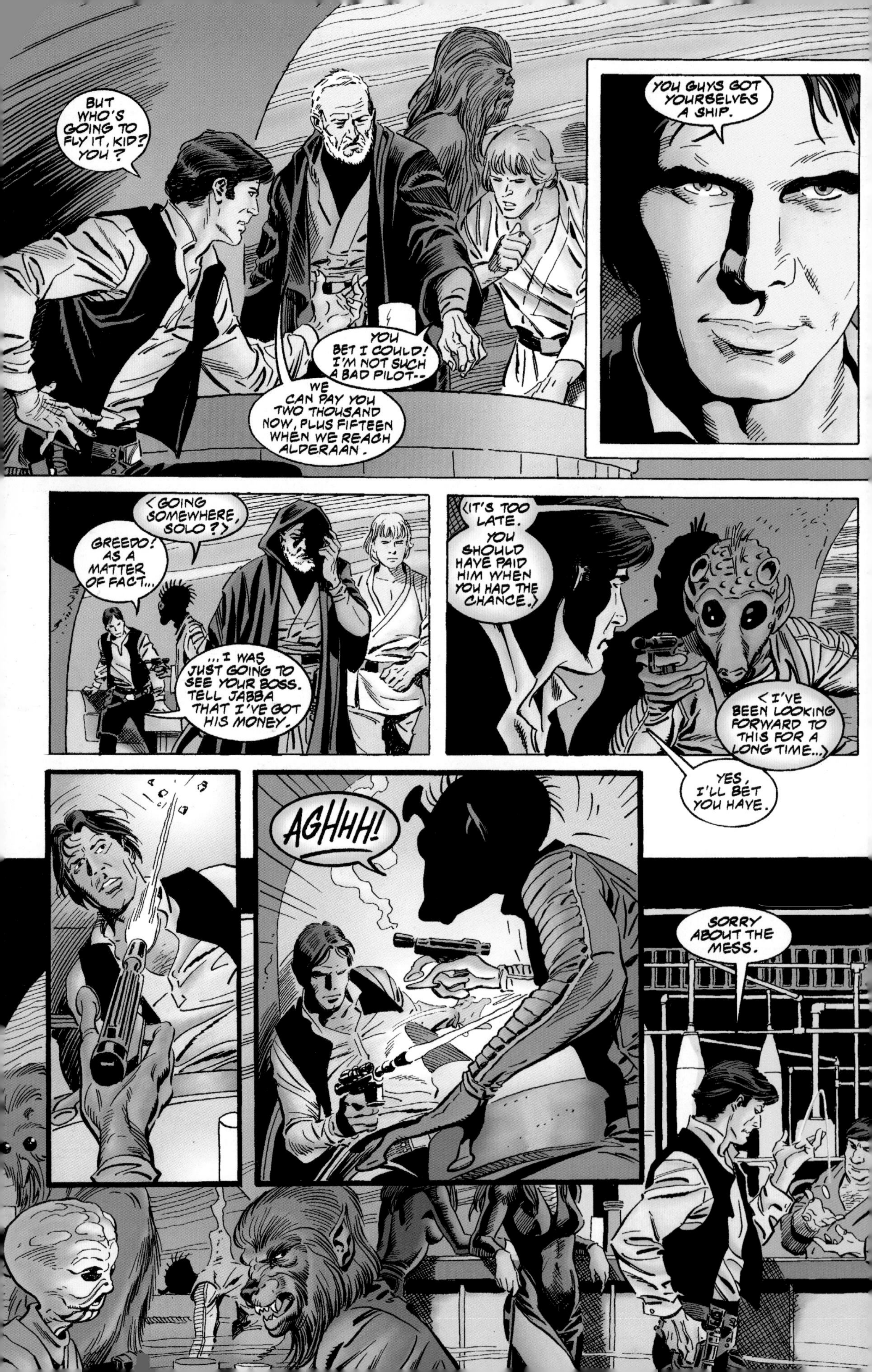
BUT WHO'S GOING TO FLY IT, KID? YOU?
YOU BET I COULD! I'M NOT SUCH A BAD PILOT--
WE CAN PAY YOU TWO THOUSAND NOW, PLUS FIFTEEN WHEN WE REACH ALDERAAN.
YOU GUYS GOT YOURSELVES A SHIP.
<GOING SOMEWHERE, SOLO?>
GREEDO! AS A MATTER OF FACT...
...I WAS JUST GOING TO SEE YOUR BOSS. TELL JABBA THAT I'VE GOT HIS MONEY.
<IT'S TOO LATE. YOU SHOULD HAVE PAID HIM WHEN YOU HAD THE CHANCE.>
<I'VE BEEN LOOKING FORWARD TO THIS FOR A LONG TIME...>
YES, I'LL BET YOU HAVE.
AGHHH!
SORRY ABOUT THE MESS.

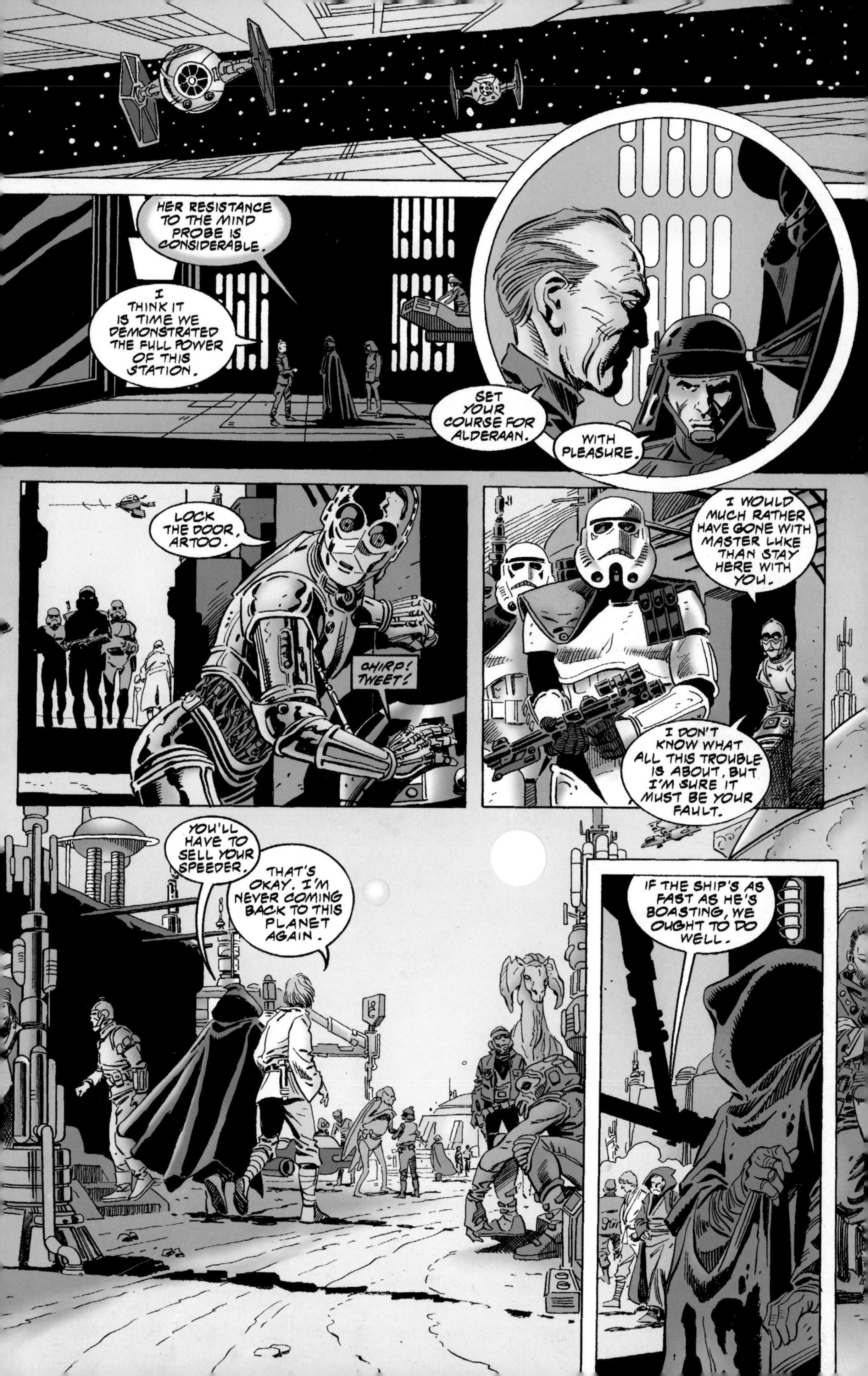
HER RESISTANCE TO THE MIND PROBE IS CONSIDERABLE.
I THINK IT IS TIME WE DEMONSTRATED THE FULL POWER OF THIS STATION.
SET YOUR COURSE FOR ALDERAAN.
WITH PLEASURE.
LOCK THE DOOR, ARTOO.
CHIRP! TWEET!
I WOULD MUCH RATHER HAVE GONE WITH MASTER LUKE THAN STAY HERE WITH YOU.
I DON'T KNOW WHAT ALL THIS TROUBLE IS ABOUT, BUT I'M SURE IT MUST BE YOUR FAULT.
YOU'LL HAVE TO SELL YOUR SPEEDER.
THAT'S OKAY. I'M NEVER COMING BACK TO THIS PLANET AGAIN.
IF THE SHIP'S AS FAST AS HE'S BOASTING, WE OUGHT TO DO WELL.

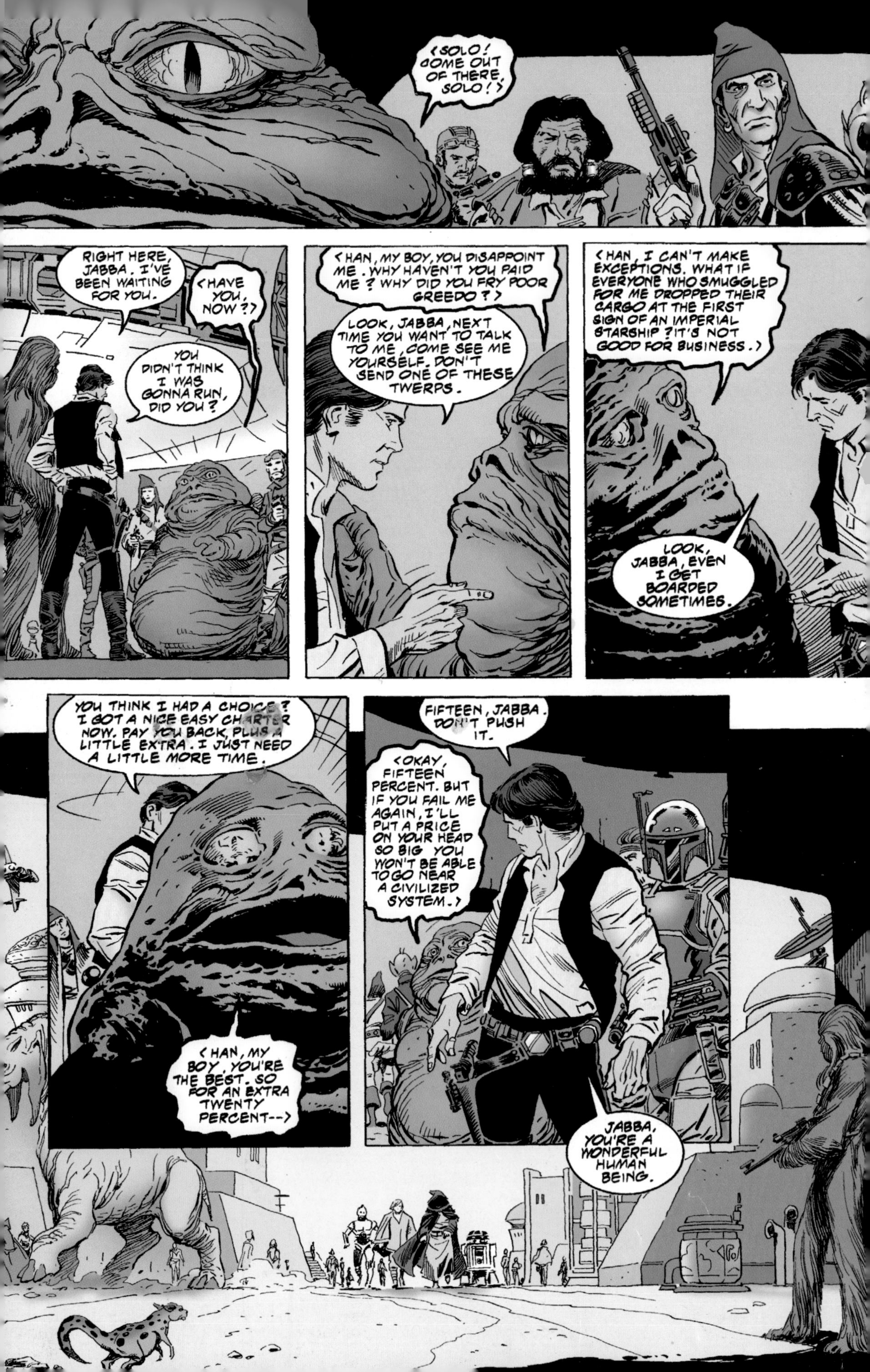

<SOLO! COME OUT OF THERE, SOLO!>
RIGHT HERE, JABBA. I'VE BEEN WAITING FOR YOU.
<HAVE YOU, NOW?>
YOU DIDN'T THINK I WAS GONNA RUN, DID YOU?
<HAN, MY BOY, YOU DISAPPOINT ME. WHY HAVEN'T YOU PAID ME? WHY DID YOU FRY POOR GREEDO?>
LOOK, JABBA, NEXT TIME YOU WANT TO TALK TO ME, COME SEE ME YOURSELF. DON'T SEND ONE OF THESE TWERPS.
<HAN, I CAN'T MAKE EXCEPTIONS. WHAT IF EVERYONE WHO SMUGGLED FOR ME DROPPED THEIR CARGO AT THE FIRST SIGN OF AN IMPERIAL STARSHIP? IT'S NOT GOOD FOR BUSINESS.>
LOOK, JABBA, EVEN I GET BOARDED SOMETIMES.
YOU THINK I HAD A CHOICE? I GOT A NICE EASY CHARTER NOW. PAY YOU BACK, PLUS A LITTLE EXTRA. I JUST NEED A LITTLE MORE TIME.
<HAN, MY BOY, YOU'RE THE BEST. SO FOR AN EXTRA TWENTY PERCENT-->
FIFTEEN, JABBA. DON'T PUSH IT.
<OKAY, FIFTEEN PERCENT. BUT IF YOU FAIL ME AGAIN, I'LL PUT A PRICE ON YOUR HEAD SO BIG YOU WON'T BE ABLE TO GO NEAR A CIVILIZED SYSTEM.>
JABBA, YOU'RE A WONDERFUL HUMAN BEING.

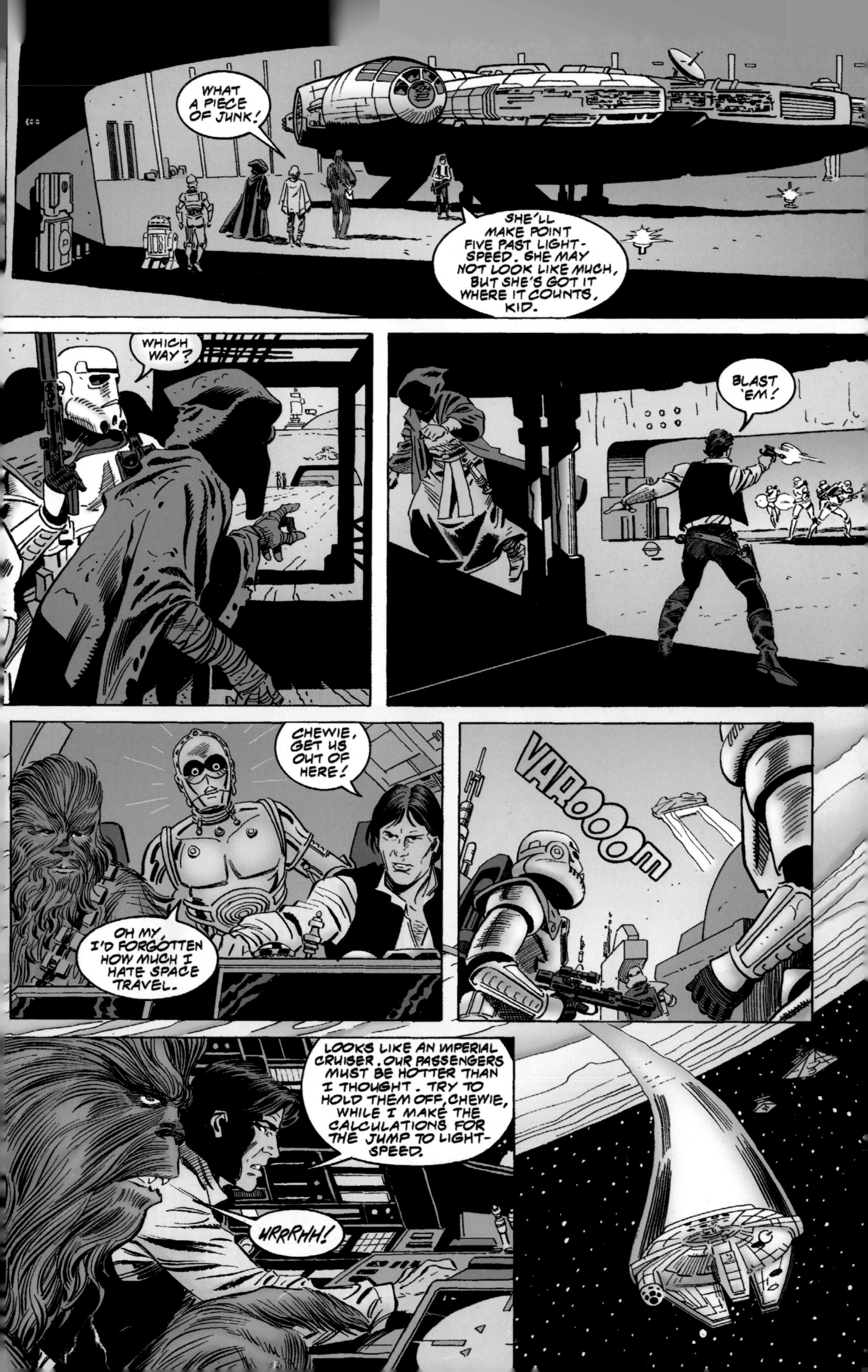
WHAT A PIECE OF JUNK!
SHE'LL MAKE POINT FIVE PAST LIGHT-SPEED. SHE MAY NOT LOOK LIKE MUCH, BUT SHE'S GOT IT WHERE IT COUNTS, KID.
WHICH WAY?
BLAST 'EM!
CHEWIE, GET US OUT OF HERE!
OH MY, I'D FORGOTTEN HOW MUCH I HATE SPACE TRAVEL.
VAROOOM
LOOKS LIKE AN IMPERIAL CRUISER. OUR PASSENGERS MUST BE HOTTER THAN I THOUGHT. TRY TO HOLD THEM OFF, CHEWIE, WHILE I MAKE THE CALCULATIONS FOR THE JUMP TO LIGHT-SPEED.
URRRHH!

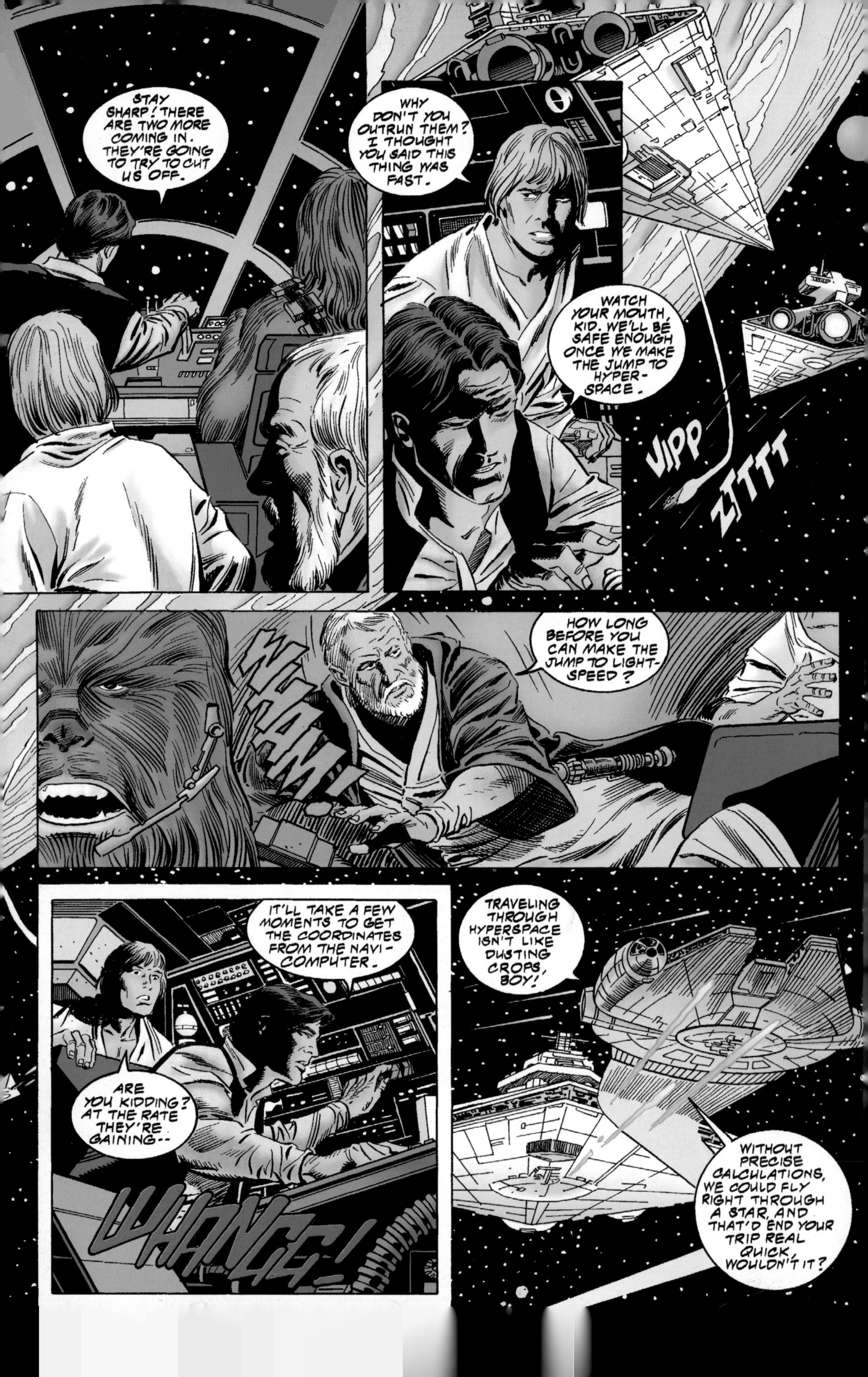

STAY SHARP! THERE ARE TWO MORE COMING IN. THEY'RE GOING TO TRY TO CUT US OFF.
WHY DON'T YOU OUTRUN THEM? I THOUGHT YOU SAID THIS THING WAS FAST.
WATCH YOUR MOUTH, KID. WE'LL BE SAFE ENOUGH ONCE WE MAKE THE JUMP TO HYPER-SPACE.
VIPP
ZTTTT
WHAM!
HOW LONG BEFORE YOU CAN MAKE THE JUMP TO LIGHT-SPEED?
IT'LL TAKE A FEW MOMENTS TO GET THE COORDINATES FROM THE NAVI-COMPUTER.
ARE YOU KIDDING? AT THE RATE THEY'RE GAINING--
WHANGG!
TRAVELING THROUGH HYPERSPACE ISN'T LIKE DUSTING CROPS, BOY!
WITHOUT PRECISE CALCULATIONS, WE COULD FLY RIGHT THROUGH A STAR, AND THAT'D END YOUR TRIP REAL QUICK, WOULDN'T IT?

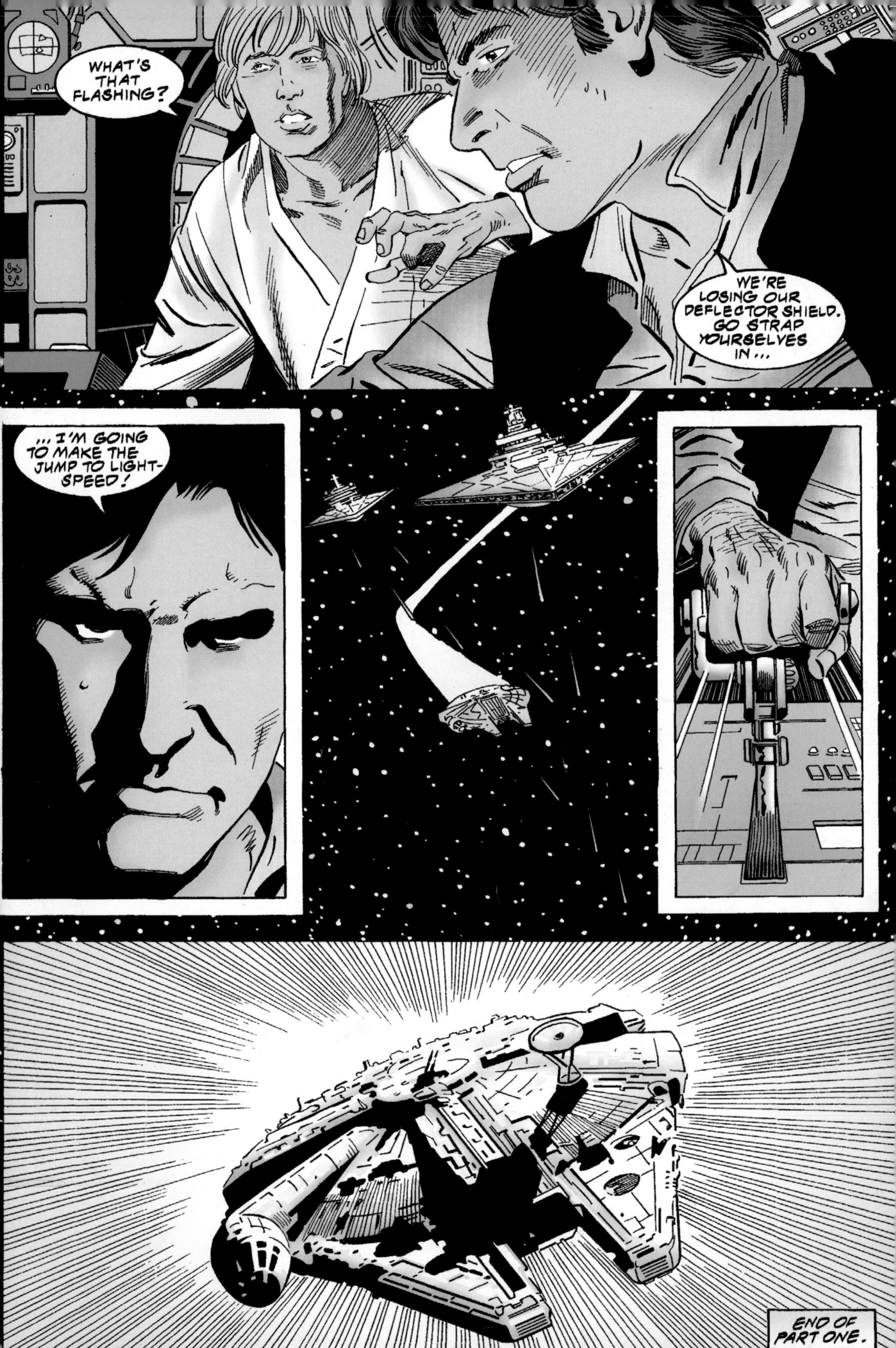
WHAT'S THAT FLASHING?
WE'RE LOSING OUR DEFLECTOR SHIELD. GO STRAP YOURSELVES IN...
...I'M GOING TO MAKE THE JUMP TO LIGHT-SPEED!
END OF PART ONE.

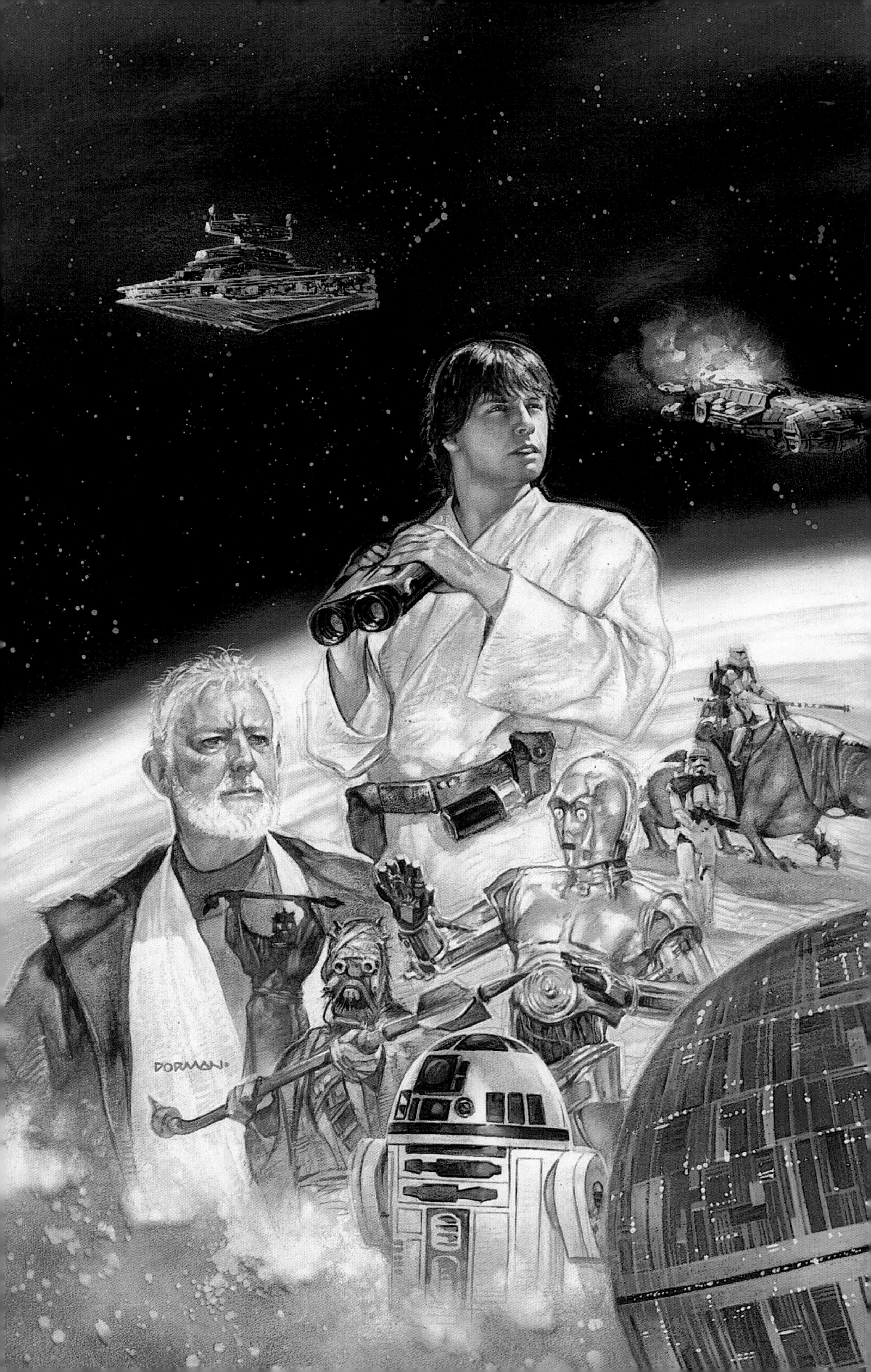
DORMAN

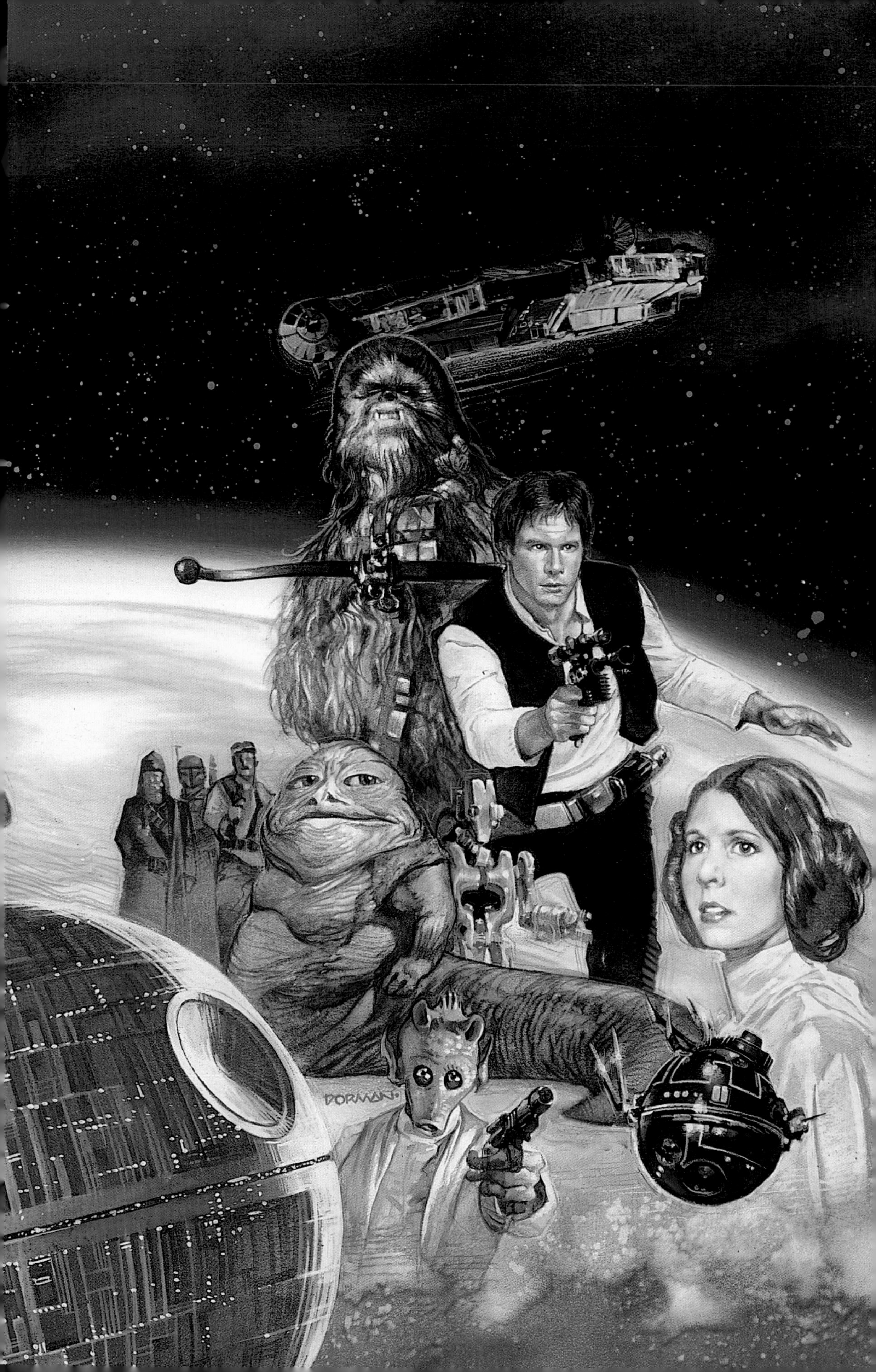
DORMAN

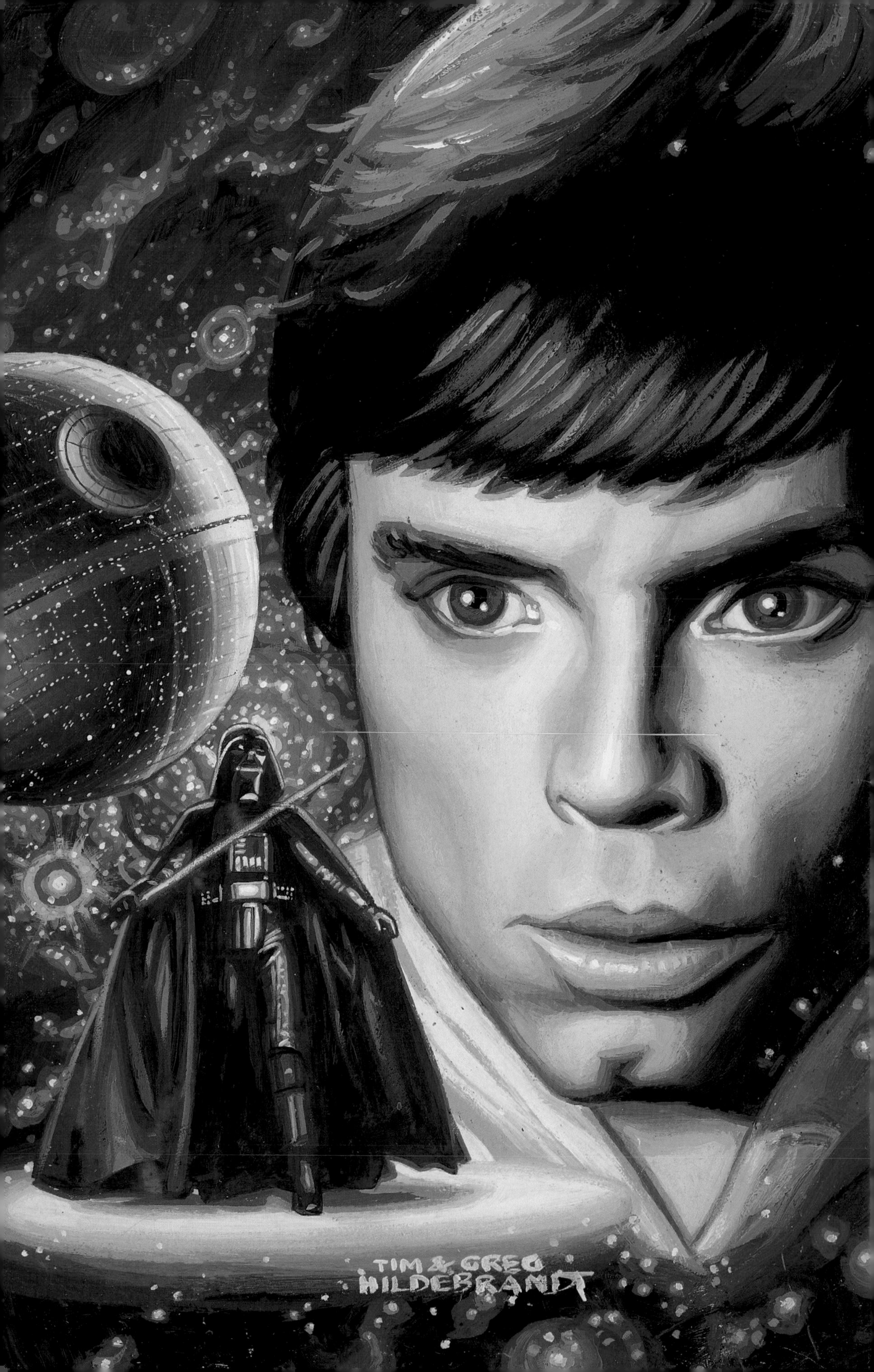
TIM & GREG
HILDEBRANDT